SIMPLE
SPEAKS
HIS MIND

SIMPLE SPEAKS HIS MIND

Langston Hughes

ÆONIAN
PRESS▲

MATTITUCK

Reprinted 1976 by Special Arrangement

International Standard Book Number 0-88411-061-3

To order contact
AEONIAN PRESS, INC.
Box 1200
Mattituck, New York 11952

Manufactured in the United States of America

To Zell and Garnett

TABLE OF CONTENTS

PART ONE

Summer Time

1

Feet Live Their Own Life

"If you want to know about my life," said Simple as he blew the foam from the top of the newly filled glass the bartender put before him, "don't look at my face, don't look at my hands. Look at my feet and see if you can tell how long I been standing on them."

"I cannot see your feet through your shoes," I said.

"You do not need to see through my shoes," said Simple. "Can't you tell by the shoes I wear—not pointed, not rocking-chair, not French-toed, not nothing but big, long, broad, and flat—that I been standing on these feet a long time and carrying some heavy burdens? They ain't flat from standing at no bar, neither, because I always sets at a bar. Can't you tell that? You know I do not hang out in a bar unless it has stools, don't you?"

"That I have observed," I said, "but I did not connect it with your past life."

"Everything I do is connected up with my past life," said Simple. "From Virginia to Joyce, from my wife to Zarita, from my mother's milk to this glass of beer, everything is connected up."

"I trust you will connect up with that dollar I just

3

loaned you when you get paid," I said. "And who is Virginia? You never told me about her."

"Virginia is where I was borned," said Simple. "I *would* be borned in a state named after a woman. From that day on, women never give me no peace."

"You, I fear, are boasting. If the women were running after you as much as you run after them, you would not be able to sit here on this bar stool in peace. I don't see any women coming to call you out to go home, as some of these fellows' wives do around here."

"Joyce better not come in no bar looking for me," said Simple. "That is why me and my wife busted up—one reason. I do not like to be called out of no bar by a female. It's a man's perogative to just set and drink sometimes."

"How do you connect that prerogative with your past?" I asked.

"When I was a wee small child," said Simple, "I had no place to set and think in, being as how I was raised up with three brothers, two sisters, seven cousins, one married aunt, a common-law uncle, and the minister's grandchild—and the house only had four rooms. I never had no place just to set and think. Neither to set and drink—not even much my milk before some hongry child snatched it out of my hand. I were not the youngest, neither a girl, nor the cutest. I don't know why, but I don't think nobody liked me much. Which is why I was afraid to like anybody for a long time myself. When I did like somebody, I was full-grown and then I picked out the wrong woman because I had no practice in liking anybody before that. We did not get along."

"Is that when you took to drink?"

"Drink took to me," said Simple. "Whiskey just naturally likes me but beer likes me better. By the time I got married I had got to the point where a cold bottle was almost as good as a warm bed, especially when the bottle could not talk and the bed-warmer could. I do not like a woman to talk to me too much—I mean about me. Which is why I like Joyce. Joyce most in generally talks about herself."

"I am still looking at your feet," I said, "and I swear they do not reveal your life to me. Your feet are no open book."

"You have eyes but you see not," said Simple. "These feet have stood on every rock from the Rock of Ages to 135th and Lenox. These feet have supported everything from a cotton bale to a hongry woman. These feet have walked ten thousand miles working for white folks and another ten thousand keeping up with colored. These feet have stood at altars, crap tables, free lunches, bars, graves, kitchen doors, betting windows, hospital clinics, WPA desks, social security railings, and in all kinds of lines from soup lines to the draft. If I just had four feet, I could have stood in more places longer. As it is, I done wore out seven hundred pairs of shoes, eighty-nine tennis shoes, twelve summer sandals, also six loafers. The socks that these feet have bought could build a knitting mill. The corns I've cut away would dull a German razor. The bunions I forgot would make you ache from now till Judgment Day. If anybody was to write the history of my life, they should start with my feet."

"Your feet are not all that extraordinary," I said. "Besides, everything you are saying is general. Tell me specifically some one thing your feet have done that makes them different from any other feet in the world, just one."

"Do you see that window in that white man's store across the street?" asked Simple. "Well, this right foot of mine broke out that window in the Harlem riots right smack in the middle. Didn't no other foot in the world break that window but mine. And this left foot carried me off running as soon as my right foot came down. Nobody else's feet saved me from the cops that night but these *two* feet right here. Don't tell me these feet ain't had a life of their own."

"For shame," I said, "going around kicking out windows. Why?"

"Why?" said Simple. "You have to ask my great-great-grandpa why. He must of been simple—else why did he let them capture him in Africa and sell him for a slave to breed my great-grandpa in slavery to breed my grandpa in slavery to breed my pa to breed me to look at that window and say, 'It ain't mine! Bam-mmm-mm-m!' and kick it out?"

"This bar glass is not yours either," I said. "Why don't you smash it?"

"It's got my beer in it," said Simple.

Just then Zarita came in wearing her Thursday-night rabbitskin coat. She didn't stop at the bar, being dressed up, but went straight back to a booth. Simple's hand went up, his beer went down, and the glass back to its wet spot on the bar.

"Excuse me a minute," he said, sliding off the stool.

Just to give him pause, the dozens, that old verbal game of maligning a friend's female relatives, came to mind.

"Wait," I said. "You have told me about what to ask your great-great-grandpa. But I want to know what to ask your great-great-grand*ma*."

"I don't play the dozens that far back," said Simple, following Zarita into the smoky juke-box blue of the back room.

2

Landladies

The next time I saw him, he was hot under the collar, but only incidentally about Zarita. Before the bartender had even put the glasses down he groaned, "I do not understand landladies."

"Now what?" I asked. "A landlady is a woman, isn't she? And, according to your declarations, you know how to handle women."

"I know how to handle women who act like ladies, but my landlady ain't no lady. Sometimes I even wish I was living with my wife again so I could have my own place and not have no landladies," said Simple.

"Landladies are practically always landladies," I said.

"But in New York they are landladies *plus!*" declared Simple.

"For instance?"

"For a instant, my landlady said to me one night when I come in, said, 'Third Floor Rear?'

"I said, 'Yes'm.'

"She says, 'You pays no attention to my notices I puts up, does you?'

"I said, 'No'm.'

"She says, 'I know you don't. You had company in your

room after ten o'clock last night in spite of my rule.'

" 'No, ma'am. That was in the room next to mine.'

" 'Yes, but you was in there with your company, Mr. Simple.' Zarita can't keep her voice down when she goes calling. 'You and you-all's company and Mr. Boyd's was raising sand. I heard you way down here.'

" 'What you heard was the Fourth Floor Back snoring, madam. We went out of here at ten-thirty and I didn't come back till two and I come back alone.'

" 'Four this morning, you mean! And you slammed the door!'

" 'Madam, you sure can hear good that late.'

" 'I am not deef. I also was raised in a decent home. And I would like you to respect my place.'

" 'Yes, ma'am,' I said, because I owed her a half week's rent and I did not want to argue right then, although I was mad. But when I went upstairs and saw that sign over them little old pink towels she hangs there in the bathroom, Lord knows for what, I got madder. Sign says:

GUEST TOWELS—ROOMERS DO NOT USE

"But when even a guest of mine uses them, she jumps salty. So for what are they there? Then I saw that other little old sign up over the sink:

WASH FACE ONLY IN BOWL—NO SOX

And a sign over the tub says:

DO NOT WASH CLOTHES IN HEAR

Another sign out in the hall says:

TURN OUT LIGHT—COSTS MONEY

As if it wasn't money I'm paying for my rent! And there's still and yet another sign in my room which states:

NO COOKING, DRINKING, NO ROWDYISMS

As if I can cook without a stove or be rowdy by myself. And then right over my bed:

NO CO. AFTER 10

Just like a man can get along in this world alone. But it were part Zarita's fault talking so loud. Anyhow when I saw all them signs I got madder than I had ever been before, and I tore them all down.

"Landladies must think roomers is uncivilized and don't know how to behave themselves. Well, I do. I was also raised in a decent home. My mama made us respect our home. And I have never been known yet to wash my socks in no face bowl. So I tore them signs down.

"The next evening when I come in from work, before I even hit the steps, the landlady yells from the parlor, 'Third Floor Rear?'

"I said, 'Yes, this is the Third Floor Rear.'

"She says, 'Does you know who tore my signs down in the bathroom and in the hall? Also your room?'

"I said, 'I tore your signs down, madam. I have been looking at them signs for three months, so I know 'em by heart.'

"She says, 'You will put them back, or else move.'

"I said, 'I not only tore them signs down, I also tore them *up!*'

"She says, 'When you have paid me my rent, you move.'

"I said, 'I will move now.'

"She said, 'You will not take your trunk now.'

"I said, 'What's to keep me?'

"She said, 'Your room door is locked.'

"I said, 'Lady, I got a date tonight. I got to get in to change my clothes.'

"She says, 'You'll get in when you pay your rent.'

"So I had to take the money for my date that night—that I was intending to take out Joyce—and pay up my room rent. The next week I didn't have enough to move, so I am still there."

"Did you put back the signs?" I asked.

"Sure," said Simple. "I even writ a new sign for her which says:

**DON'T NOBODY NO TIME TEAR DOWN
THESE SIGNS—ELSE MOVE"**

Simple Prays a Prayer

It was a hot night. Simple was sitting on his landlady's stoop reading a newspaper by streetlight. When he saw me coming, he threw the paper down.

"Good evening," I said.

"Good evening nothing," he answered. "It's too hot to be any good evening. Besides, this paper's full of nothing but atom bombs and bad news, wars and rumors of wars, airplane crashes, murders, fightings, wife-whippings, and killings from the Balkans to Brooklyn. Do you know one thing? If I was a praying man, I would pray a prayer for this world right now."

"What kind of prayer would you pray, friend?"

"I would pray a don't-want-to-have-no-more-wars prayer, and it would go like this: 'Lord,' I would say, I would ask Him, 'Lord, kindly please, take the blood off of my hands and off of my brothers' hands, and make us shake hands *clean* and not be afraid. Neither let me nor them have no knives behind our backs, Lord, nor up our sleeves, nor no bombs piled out yonder in a desert. Let's forget about bygones. Too many mens and womens are dead. The fault is mine and theirs, too. So teach us *all* to do right, Lord, *please,* and to get along together with that

12

atom bomb on this earth—because I do not want it to fall on me—nor Thee—nor anybody living. Amen!' "

"I didn't know you could pray like that," I said.

"It ain't much," said Simple, "but that girl friend of mine, Joyce, drug me to church last Sunday where the man was preaching and praying about peace, so I don't see why I shouldn't make myself up a prayer, too. I figure God will listen to me as well as the next one."

"You certainly don't have to be a minister to pray," I said, "and you have composed a good prayer. But now it's up to you to help God bring it into being, since God is created in your image."

"I thought it was the other way around," said Simple.

"However that may be," I said, "according to the Bible, God can bring things about on this earth only through man. You are a man, so you must help God make a good world."

"I am willing to help Him," said Simple, "but I do not know much what to do. The folks who run this world are going to run it in the ground in spite of all, throwing people out of work and then saying, 'Peace, it's wonderful!' Peace ain't wonderful when folks ain't got no job."

"Certainly a good job is essential to one's well-being," I said.

"It is essential to me," said Simple, "if I do not want to live off of Joyce. And I do *not* want to live off of no woman. A woman will take advantage of you, if you live off of her."

"If a woman loves you, she does not mind sharing with you," I said. "Share and share alike."

"Until times get hard!" said Simple. "But when there is not much to share, *loving* is one thing, and *sharing* is another. Often they parts company. I know because I have both loved and shared. As long as I shared *mine,* all was well, but when my wife started sharing, skippy!

"My wife said, 'Baby, when is you going to work?'

"I said, 'When I find a job.'

"She said, 'Well, it better be soon because I'm giving out.'

"And, man, I felt bad. You know how long and how hard it took to get on WPA. Many a good man lost his woman in them dark days when that stuff about 'I can't give you anything but love' didn't go far. Now it looks like love is all I am going to have to share again. Do you reckon depression days is coming back?"

"I don't know," I said. "I am not a sociologist."

"You's colleged," said Simple. "Anyhow, it looks like every time I gets a little start, something happens. I was doing right well pulling down that *fine* defense check all during the war, then all of a sudden the war had to jump up and end!"

"If you wanted the war to continue just on your account, you are certainly looking at things from a selfish viewpoint."

"Selfish!" said Simple. "You may *think* I am selfish when the facts is *I am just hongry* if I didn't have a job. It looks like in peace time nobody works as much or gets paid as much as in a war. Is that clear?"

"Clear, but not right," I said.

"Of course, it's not right to be out of work and hongry," said Simple, "just like it's not right to want to fight. That's why I prayed my prayer. I prayed for white folks, too, even though a lot of them don't believe in religion. If they did, they couldn't act the way they do.

· "Last Sunday morning when I was laying in bed drowsing and resting, I turned on the radio on my dresser and got a church—by accident. I was trying to get the Duke on records, but I turned into the wrong station. I got some white man preaching a sermon. He was talking about peace on earth, good will to men, and all such things, and he said Christ was born to bring this peace he was talking about. He said mankind has sinned! But that we have got to get ready for the Second Coming of Christ—because Christ will be back! That is what started me to wondering."

"Wondering what?" I asked.

"Wondering what all these prejudiced white folks would do if Christ did come back. I always thought Christ believed in folks' treating people right."

"He did," I said.

"Well, if He did," said Simple, "what will all these white folks do who believe in Jim Crow? Jesus said, 'Love one another,' didn't He? But they don't love me, do they?"

"Some do not," I said.

"Jesus said, 'Do unto others as you would have others do unto you.' But they don't do that way unto me, do they?"

"I suppose not," I said.

"You know not," said Simple. "They Jim Crow me and lynch me any time they want to. Suppose I was to do unto them as they does unto me? Suppose I was to lynch and Jim Crow white folks, where would I be? Huh?"

"In jail."

"You can bet your boots I would! But these are *Christian* white folks that does such things to me. At least, they call themselves Christians in my home. They got more churches down South than they got up North. They read more Bibles and sing more hymns. I hope when Christ comes back, He comes back down South. My folks need Him down there to tell them Ku Kluxers where to head in. But I'll bet you if Christ does come back, not only in the South but all over America, there would be such another running and shutting and slamming of white folks' doors in His face as you never saw! And I'll bet the Southerners couldn't get inside their Jim Crow churches fast enough to lock the gates and keep Christ out. Christ said, 'Such as ye do unto the least of these, ye do it unto me.' And Christ *knows* what these white folks have been doing to old colored me all these years."

"Of course, He knows," I said. "When Christ was here on earth, He fought for the poor and the oppressed. But some people called Him an agitator. They cursed Him and reviled Him and sent soldiers to lock Him up. They killed Him on the cross."

"At Calvary," said Simple, "way back in B.C. I know the Bible, too. My Aunt Lucy read it to me. She read how He drove the money-changers out of the Temple. Also how He changed the loaves and fishes into many and fed the poor—which made the rulers in their high places mad because they didn't want the poor to eat. Well, when Christ comes back this time, I hope He comes back *mad* His own self. I hope He drives the Jim Crowers out of their high places, every living last one of them from

Washington to Texas! I hope He smites white folks down!"

"You don't mean *all* white folks, do you?"

"No," said Simple. "I hope He lets Mrs. Roosevelt alone."

4

Conversation on the Corner

It was the summer the young men in Harlem stopped wearing their hair straightened, oiled or conked, and started having it cut short, leaving it natural, standing up about an inch or two in front in a kind of brush. When Simple took off his hat to fan his brow, I saw by the light of the neon sign outside the Wishing Well Bar that he had gotten a new haircut.

"What happened to your head?" I asked.

"Cut short," said Simple. "My baby likes to run her fingers through it. This gives her a better chance."

"As much as you hang out on this corner," I said, "I don't see when she has much of a chance."

"You know Joyce is a working woman," said Simple, "also decent. She won't come to see me, so I goes to see her early. I already paid my nightly call."

"I understand that you work also and it's midnight now. When do you sleep?"

"In between times," Simple answered, lighting a butt and taking a long draw. "Sleep don't worry me. I just hate to go back to my little old furnished room alone. How about you? What're you doing up so late?"

"Observing life for literary purposes. Gathering material, contemplating how people play so desperately when the stakes are so little."

"What you mean by all that language?" asked Simple.

"I mean there are very few people of substance out late at night—mostly hustlers. And all the hustlers around here hustle for such *small* change."

"They will not hustle off of me," said Simple. "No, sir! Somebody is always trying to take disadvantage of me. The other night I went to a poker game and lost Twelve Bucks. They was playing partners, dealing seconds, stripping the deck and palming, so all I could do was lose. I could not win—so I prefer to drink it up."

"At least you'll have it *in* you," I said. "But why do you imbibe practically every night?"

"Because I like it. I also drink because I don't have anything better to do."

"Why don't you read a book," I asked, "go to a show or a dance?"

"I do not read a book because I don't understand books, daddy-o. I do not go to the show because you see nothing but white folks on the screen. And I do not go to a dance because if I do, I get in trouble with Joyce, who is one girl friend I respect."

"Trouble with Joyce?"

"Yes," said Simple, leaning on the mailbox so no one could mail a letter. "Joyce thinks every time I put my arms around a woman to dance with her, I am hugging the woman! Now, how can you dance with a woman without hugging her? I see Joyce enough as it is. I drink because I am lonesome."

"Lonesome? How can you be lonesome when you've got plenty of friends, also girl friends?"

"I'm lonesome inside myself."

"How do you explain that?"

"I do not know," said Simple, "but that is why I drink. I don't do nobody no harm, do I? You don't see me out here hustling off nobody, do you? I am not mugging and cheating and robbing, am I?"

"You're not."

"So I don't see why I shouldn't take a beer now and then."

"*When* did you say?"

"Now," said Simple.

"You said 'now and then,' which is putting it mildly."

"I meant *now*," said Simple, "*right now* since I have met up with you, old buddy, and I know you will buy a beer."

"I saw Zarita in that bar," I said, "and if we go in there, you will have to buy her more than a beer."

"No, I won't! I'm off that dame. She talks too loud—come near getting me put out of my room. Besides, she will drink you up coming and going and not try to pay you back in no way. She is one of them hustlers you was talking about always out in the street at blip-A.M."

"Most of these people where you hang out are hustlers."

"All but you and me. I came out here hoping to run across you to borrow a fin until payday."

"I regret to say that I don't have anything to lend."

"Too bad—because I was going to buy you a drink."

"Then lose the rest in a game?"

"I was not," said Simple. "You see that cat inside the

bar with that long fingernail, don't you? Well, he uses that nail to mark cards with. Every time I get in a game, there is somebody dealing with a *long* fingernail. It ain't safe! I am tired of trickeration. Also I have had too many hypes laid down on me. Now I am hep."

"I'm glad to hear that," I said. "It's about time you settled down anyhow and married Joyce."

"Right. I would marry her," said Simple, "except that that girl insists that I get a divorce first. But my wife won't pay for it. And looks like I can't get that much dough ahead myself—in my line of work, I can't grow no long fingernails because they would break off before night."

"Oh, so you would like to be a hustler, too."

"Only until I pay for my divorce from Isabel," said Simple.

"If you hadn't quit your wife, you wouldn't need a divorce," I said. "If I had a wife, *I* would stay with her."

"You have never been married, pal, so you do not know how hard it is sometimes to stay with a wife."

"Elucidate," I said, "while we go in the bar and have a beer."

"A wife you have to take with a grain of salt," Simple explained. "But sometimes the salt runs out."

"What do you mean by that parable?"

"Don't take serious everything a wife says. I did. For instant, I believed her when my wife said, 'Baby, I don't mind you going out. I know a man has to get out sometimes and he don't want his wife running with him everywhere he goes.'

"So I went out. I didn't take her. She got mad. I should have taken that with a grain of salt. Also take money. My

wife said, 'A man is due to have his own spending change.'
So every week I kept Five Dollars out of my salary. When
that ran out 'long toward the end of the week, and I would
ask Isabel for a quarter or so, she'd say, 'What did you
do with that Five Dollars?'

"I'd say, 'I spent it.'

" 'Spent it on what?' she'd say.

" 'I drunk it up.'

" 'What did you do that for?' she'd yell. 'Why didn't
you have your clothes pressed, or spend it on some good
books?'

" 'I didn't want any good books.'

" 'Why didn't you send some of it to your old aunt?'

" 'Next time I will *tell* you that I sent it *all* to my old
aunt.'

" 'Then you intend to lie to me?' says my wife.

" 'Anything to keep down an argument,' I says.

" 'You do not trust me,' Isabel hollers. Then she starts
to quarrel. So you see how it is. A woman will get you
going and coming. You can't outargue a woman. She even
had the nerve to tell me, 'Why don't you buy your beer by
the case and set up home here and drink it with me?'

"I said, 'Baby, I cannot set up here at home and look
into your face each and every night.'

"She said, 'You took me for better or worse. Do I look
worse to you now?'

"I said, 'You do not look any worse, baby, but neither
does you look any better as time goes on.'

"She said, 'If you would buy me some clothes, maybe I
could look like something.'

"I said, 'Honey, we ain't got our furniture paid for yet.'

"She said, 'So you care more for an old kitchen stove than you does for me?'

"I said, 'A man has to eat, and a woman can't cook on the floor.'

" 'All you got me for is to cook,' Isabel said. 'If I had knowed that, I could of stayed home with my mother.'

" 'I must admit,' I said, 'your mother cooks better than you.'

" 'Huh! I can't do nothing with them stringy old round steaks you bring home for us to eat,' she says.

" 'My money won't stretch to no T-bones,' I says. 'Anyhow, baby, no matter how tough the steak may be, you can always stick a fork in the gravy.'

"I just said that for a joke, but somehow it made her mad. She flew off the handle. I flew off the handle, too, and we had one of the biggest quarrels you ever saw. Our first battle royal—but it were not our last. Every time night fell from then on we quarreled—and night falls every night in Baltimore."

"Night does," I said.

"The first of the month falls every month, too, North or South. And them white folks who sends bills never forgets to send them—the phone bill, the furniture bill, the water bill, the gas bill, insurance, house rent. They also never forget you got their furniture in the house—and they will come and take it out if you do not pay the bill. Not only was my nose kept to the grindstone when I was married, but my bohunkus also. It were depression, too. They cut my wages down once at the foundry. They cut my wages down again. Then they cut my wages *out*, also the job. My old lady had to go cook for some rich white folks. *And*

*don't you know Isabel wouldn't bring me home a thing
to eat!* Neither would she open a can when she got home.

"I said, 'Baby, what is the matter with you? Don't you
know I have to eat, too?'

"She said, 'You know what is the matter with me. Ever
since I have been with you, I have been treated like a dog
for convenience. Who is paying for this furniture? Me!
Who keeps up the house rent? Me! Who pays that little
dime insurance of yourn? Me! And if you was to die, I
would not benefit but Three Hundred Dollars. It looks like
you can't even get on WPA. But you better get on something, Jess. In fact, take over or take off.'

"Then it were that I took off," said Simple.

"And ever since you've been a free man."

"Free?" said Simple. "I would have been free if I hadn't
run into some old Baltimore friend boy here in Harlem
who wrote and told my wife where I was at. So for the
last year now she's been writing me that if I wasn't going
to even give her a divorce, to at least buy her a fur coat
this winter."

"Why didn't you give her a divorce when you left?" I
asked.

"You can't buy no divorce on WPA. And when the war
came, she was working in a war plant making just as much
money as me," said Simple. "She could get her own
divorce. But no! She still wanted me to pay for it. I told
her to send me the money then and I would pay for it. But
she wrote back and said I would never spend none of her
money on Joyce. Baltimore womens is evil."

"Evidently she does not trust you."

"I would not trust myself with Three Hundred Dollars," said Simple.

"So you are just going to keep on being married then. You can't get loose if neither one of you is willing to pay for the divorce."

"I've been trying to get Joyce to pay for it," explained Simple. "Only thing is, Joyce says I will have to marry her *first*. She says she will not pay for no divorce for another woman unless I am hers beforehand."

"That would be bigamy," I said, "married to two women at once."

"It would be worse than that," said Simple. "Married to one woman is bad enough. But if I am married to two, it would be hell!"

"Legally it would be bigamy."

"Is bigamy worse than hell?"

"I have had no experience with either," I said. "But if you go in for bigamy, you will end up in the arms of justice."

"Any old arms are better than none," said Simple.

5

Family Tree

"Anybody can look at me and tell I am part Indian," said Simple.

"I see you almost every day," I said, "and I did not know it until now."

"I have Indian blood but I do not show it much," said Simple. "My uncle's cousin's great-grandma were a Cherokee. I only shows mine when I lose my temper—then my Indian blood boils. I am quick-tempered just like a Indian. If somebody does something to me, I always fights back. In fact, when I get mad, I am the toughest Negro God's got. It's my Indian blood. When I were a young man, I used to play baseball and steal bases just like Jackie. If the empire would rule me out, I would get mad and hit the empire. I had to stop playing. That Indian temper. Nowadays, though, it's mostly womens that riles me up, especially landladies, waitresses, and girl friends. To tell the truth, I believe in a woman keeping her place. Womens is beside themselves these days. They want to rule the roost."

"You have old-fashioned ideas about sex," I said. "In fact, your line of thought is based on outmoded economics."

"What?"

"In the days when women were dependent upon men for a living, you could be the boss. But now women make their own living. Some of them make more money than you do."

"True," said Simple. "During the war they got into that habit. But boss I am still due to be."

"So you think. But you can't always put your authority into effect."

"I can try," said Simple. "I can say, 'Do this!' And if she does something else, I can raise my voice, if not my hand."

"You can be sued for raising your voice," I stated, "and arrested for raising your hand."

"And she can be annihilated when I return from being arrested," said Simple. "That's my Indian blood!"

"You must believe in a woman being a squaw."

"She better not look like no squaw," said Simple. "I want a woman to look sharp when she goes out with me. No moccasins. I wants high-heel shoes and nylons, cute legs—and short dresses. But I also do not want her to talk back to me. As I said, I am the man. *Mine* is the word, and she is due to hush."

"Indians customarily expect their women to be quiet," I said.

"I do not expect mine to be *too* quiet," said Simple. "I want 'em to sweet-talk me—'Sweet baby, this,' and 'Baby, that,' and 'Baby, you's right, darling,' when they talk to me."

"In other words, you want them both old-fashioned and modern at the same time," I said. "The convolutions of your hypothesis are sometimes beyond cognizance."

"Cog hell!" said Simple. "I just do not like no old loud back-talking chick. That's the Indian in me. My grandpa on my father's side were like that, too, an Indian. He was married five times and he really ruled his roost."

"There are a mighty lot of Indians up your family tree," I said. "Did your granddad look like one?"

"Only his nose. He was dark brownskin otherwise. In fact, he were black. And the womens! Man! They was crazy about Grandpa. Every time he walked down the street, they stuck their heads out the windows and kept 'em turned South—which was where the beer parlor was."

"So your grandpa was a drinking man, too. That must be whom you take after."

"I also am named after him," said Simple. "Grandpa's name was Jess, too. So I am Jesse B. Semple."

"What does the *B* stand for?"

"Nothing. I just put it there myself since they didn't give me no initial when I was born. I am really Jess Semple —which the kids changed around into a nickname when I were in school. In fact, they used to tease me when I were small, calling me 'Simple Simon.' But I was right handy with my fists, and after I beat the 'Simon' out of a few of them, they let me alone. But my friends still call me 'Simple.' "

"In reality, you are Jesse Semple," I said, "colored."

"Part Indian," insisted Simple, reaching for his beer.

"Jess is certainly not an Indian name."

"No, it ain't," said Simple, "but we did have a Hiawatha in our family. She died."

"*She?*" I said. "Hiawatha was no *she*."

"She was a *she* in our family. And she had long coal-black hair just like a Creole. You know, I started to marry a Creole one time when I was coach-boy on the L. & N. down to New Orleans. Them Louisiana girls are bee-oou-te-ful! Man, I mean!"

"Why didn't you marry her, fellow?"

"They are more dangerous than a Indian," said Simple, "also I do not want no pretty woman. First thing you know, you fall in love with her—then you got to kill somebody about her. She'll make you so jealous, you'll bust! A pretty woman will get a man in trouble. Me and my Indian blood, quick-tempered as I is. No! I do not crave a pretty woman."

"Joyce is certainly not bad-looking," I said. "You hang around her all the time."

"She is far from a Creole. Besides, she appreciates me," said Simple. "Joyce knows I got Indian blood which makes my temper bad. But we take each other as we is. I respect her and she respects me."

"That's the way it should be with the whole world," I said. "Therefore, you and Joyce are setting a fine example in these days of trials and tribulations. Everybody should take each other as they are, white, black, Indians, Creole. Then there would be no prejudice, nations would get along."

"Some folks do not see it like that," said Simple. "For instant, my landlady—and my wife. Isabel could never get along with me. That is why we are not together to-day."

"I'm not talking personally," I said, "so why bring in your wife?"

"Getting along *starts* with persons, don't it?" asked

Simple. "You *must* include my wife. That woman got my Indian blood so riled up one day I thought I would explode."

"I still say, I'm not talking personally."

"Then stop talking," exploded Simple, "because with me it is personal. Facts, I cannot even talk about my wife if I don't get personal. That's how it is if you're part Indian—everything is personal. *Heap much personal.*"

6

A Toast to Harlem

Quiet can seem unduly loud at times. Since nobody at the bar was saying a word during a lull in the bright blues-blare of the Wishing Well's usually overworked juke box, I addressed my friend Simple.

"Since you told me last night you are an Indian, explain to me how it is you find yourself living in a furnished room in Harlem, my brave buck, instead of on a reservation?"

"I am a colored Indian," said Simple.

"In other words, a Negro."

"A Black Foot Indian, daddy-o, not a red one. Anyhow, Harlem is the place I always did want to be. And if it wasn't for landladies, I would be happy. That's a fact! I love Harlem."

"What is it you love about Harlem?"

"It's so full of Negroes," said Simple. "I feel like I got protection."

"From what?"

"From white folks," said Simple. "Furthermore, I like Harlem because it belongs to me."

"Harlem does not belong to you. You don't own the houses in Harlem. They belong to white folks."

"I might not own 'em," said Simple, "but I live in 'em. It would take an atom bomb to get me out."

"Or a depression," I said.

"I would not move for no depression. No, I would not go back down South, not even to Baltimore. I am in Harlem to stay! You say the houses ain't mine. Well, the sidewalk is—and don't nobody push me off. The cops don't even say, 'Move on,' hardly no more. They learned something from them Harlem riots. They used to beat your head right in public, but now they only beat it after they get you down to the stationhouse. And they don't beat it then if they think you know a colored congressman."

"Harlem has a few Negro leaders," I said.

"Elected by my *own* vote," said Simple. "Here I ain't scared to vote—that's another thing I like about Harlem. I also like it because we've got subways and it does not take all day to get downtown, neither are you Jim Crowed on the way. Why, Negroes is running some of these subway trains. This morning I rode the A Train down to 34th Street. There were a Negro driving it, making ninety miles a hour. That cat *were really driving* that train! Every time he flew by one of them local stations looks like he was saying, 'Look at me! This train is mine!' That cat were gone, ole man. Which is another reason why I like Harlem! Sometimes I run into Duke Ellington on 125th Street and I say, 'What you know there, Duke?' Duke says, 'Solid, ole man.' He does not know me from Adam, but he speaks. One day I saw Lena Horne coming out of the Hotel Theresa and I said, 'Huba! Huba!' Lena smiled. Folks is friendly in Harlem. I feel like I got the world in a jug and the stopper in my hand! So drink a toast to Harlem!"

Simple lifted his glass of beer:

> *"Here's to Harlem!*
> *They say Heaven is Paradise.*
> *If Harlem ain't Heaven,*
> *Then a mouse ain't mice!"*

"Heaven is a state of mind," I commented.

"It sure is *mine*," said Simple, draining his glass. "From Central Park to 179th, from river to river, Harlem is mine! Lots of white folks is scared to come up here, too, after dark."

"That is nothing to be proud of," I said.

"I am sorry white folks is scared to come to Harlem, but I am scared to go around some of *them*. Why, for instant, in my home town once before I came North to live, I was walking down the street when a white woman jumped out of her door and said, 'Boy, get away from here because I am scared of you.'

"I said, 'Why?'

"She said, 'Because you are black.'

"I said, 'Lady, I am scared of you because you are white.' I went on down the street, but I kept wishing I was blacker—so I could of scared that lady to death. So help me, I did. Imagine somebody talking about they is scared of me because I am black! I got more reason to be scared of white folks than they have of me."

"Right," I said.

"The white race drug me over here from Africa, slaved

me, freed me, lynched me, starved me during the depression, Jim Crowed me during the war—then they come talking about they is scared of me! Which is why I am glad I have got one spot to call my own where I hold sway—Harlem. Harlem, where I can thumb my nose at the world!"

"You talk just like a Negro nationalist," I said.

"What's that?"

"Someone who wants Negroes to be on top."

"When everybody else keeps me on the *bottom*, I don't see why I shouldn't want to be on top. I will, too, someday."

"That's the spirit that causes wars," I said.

"I would not mind a war if I could win it. White folks fight, lynch, and enjoy themselves."

"There you go," I said. "That old *race-against-race* jargon. There'll never be peace that way. The world tomorrow ought to be a world where everybody gets along together. The least we can do is extend a friendly hand."

"Every time I extend my hand I get put back in my place. You know them poetries about the black cat that tried to be friendly with the white one:

> *The black cat said to the white cat,*
> *'Let's sport around the town.'*
> *The white cat said to the black cat,*
> *'You better set your black self down!'* "

"Unfriendliness of that nature should not exist," I said. "Folks ought to live like neighbors."

"You're talking about what ought to be. But as long

as what *is* is—and Georgia is Georgia—I will take Harlem for mine. At least, if trouble comes, I will have *my own window* to shoot from."

"I refuse to argue with you any more," I said. "What Harlem ought to hold out to the world from its windows is a friendly hand, not a belligerent attitude."

"It will not be my attitude I will have out my window," said Simple.

7

Simple and His Sins

Just as the street lights were coming on one warm Sunday evening in midsummer, I ran into my friend of the bar stools between Paddy's and the Wishing Well. He was wiping his brow.

"Man, I came near getting my wires crossed this afternoon," he said, "and all by accident. I told Joyce I would meet her in the park, so I was setting out there on a bench with my portable radio just bugging myself with Dizzy Gillespie, when who should come blaséing along but Zarita."

"How did she look by daylight?" I asked.

"She looked fine from the bottom up, but beat from the top down," said Simple.

"You kept your eyes down, I presume."

"No, I didn't neither," said Simple. "I looked Zarita dead in the eye and I said, 'Woman, what you doing out here in the broad-open daytime with your head looking like Zip?'

"Zarita said, 'Don't look at my hair, Jess, please. I ain't been to the beauty shop this week.'

" 'Then you ought to go,' I said. 'Besides, how are you going to get your rest staying up all night? Last thing I saw last night was you—and now you're out here in the park and it ain't hardly noon.'

· " 'I could ask you the same thing,' said Zarita, 'but I ain't that concerned about your business. And I don't have to answer your questions.'

" 'You didn't mind answering them last night when I was buying you all them drinks,' I said.

" 'To be a gentleman,' said Zarita, 'you speaks too often about the money you spend. I'll bet you if your girl friend ever saw you setting up in the bar having a ball every A.M. she would lay you low.'

" 'Joyce knows all about me,' I said, 'and I would thank you to keep her name out of this. Joyce is a lady.'

" 'What do you think I am?' yells Zarita.

" 'You ain't even an imitation,' I said, 'coming out in the street with your head looking like a hurrah's nest!' "

"Why were you so hard on Zarita?" I asked. "I thought she was a friend of yours."

"She ain't nothing but a night-time friend," said Simple, "and I do not like to see her in the day. You would not like to see her neither if you had seen her this noon. I often wonders what makes some women look so bad early in the day after they have looked so sweet at night. Can you tell me?"

"You can answer that yourself."

"Well, for one thing, a woman is half make-up," said Simple, "and the other half is clothes. They got no business coming out in the morning before they fix themselves up. I said, 'Zarita, go on home and put on some face, also oil your meriney.'

" 'I can see through you,' she hollered. 'You just scared

somebody will spy you talking to me out here in the broad daylight and go tell that female friend of yourn. Well, you ain't gonna drive me off with your insulting remarks. This is a public park. I aims to set right here on this bench with you, Jess Simple, and listen to that radio until the Dodgers come on. I follows Jackie.'

" 'You will have to follow Jackie on somebody else's radio,' I said. 'I will not be seen setting in the park with no uncombed woman. Neither do I know you that well, Zarita, for you to set down here with me.'

" 'I set on a bar stool with you,' says Zarita.

" 'Not on the same stool,' I says. 'Woman, unhand me and lemme go.'

"Don't you know I had trouble getting away from that girl. Zarita pitched a boogie right there in the park and she has got a voice like a steam calliope. I cut out and went up to Joyce's house.

"When I rung Joyce's bell, she comes to the door in her wrapper and says, 'Baby, I thought you was going to set in the park until I got dressed.'

"I said, 'Joyce, you took too long. Let's go to a nice air-cooled movie instead of setting in the park listening to the ball game today. I hear Jackie's twisted his ankle, anyhow.' And I put that radio down and took that woman the other way, so she would not run into Zarita."

"Your sins will find you out," I said.

"I don't care nothing about my sins finding me out," said Simple, "just so Joyce don't find out about my sins—especially when their hair ain't combed."

8

Temptation

"When the Lord said, 'Let there be light,' and there was light, what I want to know is where was us colored people?"

"What do you mean, 'Where were we colored people?' " I said.

"We must *not* of been there," said Simple, "because we are still dark. Either He did not include me or else I were not there."

"The Lord was not referring to people when He said, 'Let there be light.' He was referring to the elements, the atmosphere, the air."

"He must have included some people," said Simple, "because white people are light, in fact, *white,* whilst I am dark. How come? I say, we were not there."

"Then where do you think we were?"

"Late as usual," said Simple, "old C. P. Time. We must have been down the road a piece and did not get back on time."

"There was no C. P. Time in those days," I said. "In fact, no people were created—so there couldn't be any Colored People's Time. The Lord God had not yet breathed the breath of life into anyone."

"No?" said Simple.

"No," said I, "because it wasn't until Genesis 2 and 7 that God 'formed man of the dust of the earth and breathed into his nostrils the breath of life and man became a living soul.' His name was Adam. Then He took one of Adam's ribs and made a woman."

"Then trouble began," said Simple. "Thank God, they was both white."

"How do you know Adam and Eve were white?" I asked.

"When I was a kid I seen them on the Sunday school cards," said Simple. "Ever since I been seeing a Sunday school card, they was white. That is why I want to know where was us Negroes when the Lord said, 'Let there be light'?"

"Oh, man, you have a color complex so bad you want to trace it back to the Bible."

"No, I don't. I just want to know how come Adam and Eve was white. If they had started out black, this world might not be in the fix it is today. Eve might not of paid that serpent no attention. I never did know a Negro yet that liked a snake."

"That snake is a symbol," I said, "a symbol of temptation and sin. And that symbol would be the same, no matter what the race."

"I am not talking about no symbol," said Simple. "I am talking about the day when Eve took that apple and Adam et. From then on the human race has been in trouble. There ain't a colored woman living what would take no apple from a snake—and she better not give no snake-apples to her husband!"

"Adam and Eve are symbols, too," I said.

"You are simple yourself," said Simple. "But I just wish we colored folks had been somewhere around at the start. I do not know where we was when Eden was a garden, but we sure didn't get in on none of the crops. If we had, we would not be so poor today. White folks started out ahead and they are still ahead. Look at me!"

"I am looking," I said.

"Made in the image of God," said Simple, "but I never did see anybody like me on a Sunday school card."

"Probably nobody looked like you in Biblical days," I said. "The American Negro did not exist in B.C. You're a product of Caucasia and Africa, Harlem and Dixie. You've been conditioned entirely by our environment, our modern times."

"Times have been hard," said Simple, "but still I am a child of God."

"In the cosmic sense, we are all children of God."

"I have been baptized," said Simple, "also anointed with oil. When I were a child I come through at the mourners' bench. I was converted. I have listened to Daddy Grace and et with Father Divine, moaned with Elder Lawson and prayed with Adam Powell. Also I have been to the Episcopalians with Joyce. But if a snake were to come up to me and offer *me* an apple, I would say, 'Varmint, be on your way! No fruit today! Bud, you got the wrong stud now, so get along somehow, be off down the road because you're lower than a toad!' Then that serpent would respect me as a wise man—and this world would not be where it is—all on account of an apple. That apple has turned into an atom now."

"To hear you talk, if you had been in the Garden of Eden, the world would still be a Paradise," I said. "Man would not have fallen into sin."

"Not *this* man," said Simple. "I would have stayed in that garden making grape wine, singing like Crosby, and feeling fine! I would not be scuffling out in this rough world, neither would I be in Harlem. If I was Adam I would just stay in Eden in that garden with no rent to pay, no landladies to dodge, no time clock to punch—and *my* picture on a Sunday school card. I'd be a *real gone guy* even if I didn't have but one name—Adam—and no initials."

"You would be *real gone* all right. But you were not there. So, my dear fellow, I trust you will not let your rather late arrival on our contemporary stage distort your perspective."

"No," said Simple.

9

Wooing the Muse

"Hey, now!" said Simple one hot Monday evening. "Man, I had a *fine* weekend."

"What did you do?"

"Me and Joyce went to Orchard Beach."

"Good bathing?"

"I don't know. I didn't take a bath. I don't take to cold water."

"What did you do then, just lie in the sun?"

"I did not," said Simple. "I don't like violent rays tampering with my complexion. I just laid back in the shade while Joyce sported on the beach wetting her toes to show off her pretty white bathing suit."

"In other words, you relaxed."

"Relaxed is right," said Simple. "I had myself a great big nice cool quart of beer so I just laid back in the shade and relaxed. I also wrote myself some poetries."

"Poetry!" I said.

"Yes," said Simple. "Want to hear it?"

"Indeed I do."

"I will read you Number One. Here it is:

> *Sitting under the trees*
> *With the birds and the bees*
> *Watching the girls go by.*

How do you like it?"

"Is that all?"

"That's enough!" said Simple.

"You ought to have another rhyme," I said. *"By* ought to rhyme with *sky* or something."

"I was not looking at no sky, as I told you in the poem. I was looking at the girls."

"Well, anyhow, what else did you write?"

"This next one is a killer," said Simple. "It's serious. I got to thinking about how if I didn't have to ride Jim Crow, I might go down home for my vacation. And I looked around me out yonder at Orchard Beach and almost everybody on that beach, besides me and Joyce, was foreigners—New York foreigners. They was speaking Italian, German, Yiddish, Spanish, Puerto Rican, and everything but English. So I got to thinking how any one of them foreigners could visit my home state down South and ride anywhere they want to on the trains—except with me. So I wrote this poem which I will now read it to you. Listen:

> *I wonder how it can be*
> *That Greeks, Germans, Jews,*
> *Italians, Mexicans,*
> *And everybody but me*
> *Down South can ride in the trains,*
> *Streetcars and busses*
> *Without any fusses.*
>
> *But when I come along—*
> *Pure American—*

They got a sign up
For me to ride behind:

COLORED

My folks and my folks' folkses
And their folkses before
Have been here 300 years or more—
Yet any foreigner from Polish to Dutch
Rides anywhere he wants to
And is not subject to such
Treatments as my fellow-men give me
In this Land of the Free.

Dixie, you ought to get wise
And be civilized!
And take down that COLORED sign
For Americans to ride behind!

Signed, *Jesse B. Semple.* How do you like that?"

"Did you write it yourself, or did Joyce help you?"

"Every word of it I writ myself," said Simple. "Joyce wanted me to change *folkses* and say *peoples,* but I did not have an eraser. It would have been longer, too, but Joyce made me stop and go with her to get some hot dogs."

"It's long enough," I said.

"It's not as long as Jim Crow," said Simple.

"You didn't write any nature poems at all?" I asked.

"What do you mean, nature poems?"

"I mean about the great out-of-doors—the flowers, the birds, the trees, the country."

"To tell the truth, I never was much on country," said Simple. "I had enough of it when I was down home. Besides, in the country flies bother you, bees sting you, mosquitoes bite you, and snakes hide in the grass. No, I do not like the country—except a riverbank to fish near town."

"It's better than staying in the city," I said, "and spending your money around these Harlem bars."

"At least I am welcome in these bars—run by white folks though they are," said Simple, "but I do not know no place in the country where I am welcome. If you're driving, every little roadhouse you stop at, they look at you like you was a varmint and say, 'We don't serve colored.' I tell you I do not want no parts of the country in this country."

"You do not go to the country to drink," I said.

"What am I gonna do, hibernate?"

"You could lie in a hammock and read a book, then go in the house and eat chicken."

"I do not know anybody in the country around here, and you know these summer resort places up North don't admit colored. Besides, the last time I was laying out in a hammock reading the funnies in the country down in Virginia, it were in the cool of evening and, man, a snake as long as you are tall come whipping through the grass, grabbed a frog right in front of my eyes, and started to choking it down."

"What did you do?"

"Mighty near fell out of that hammock!" said Simple. "If that snake had not been so near, I would've fell out.

As it were, I stepped down quick on the other side and went to find myself a stone."

"Did you kill it?"

"My nerves were bad and my aim was off. I hit the frog instead of the snake. I knocked that frog right out of his mouth."

"What did the snake do?"

"Runned and hid his self in the grass. I was scared to go outdoors all the rest of the time I was in the country."

"You are that scared of a snake?" I said.

"As scared of a snake as a Russian was of a Nazi. I would go to as much trouble to kill one as Stalin did to kill Hitler. Besides, that poor little frog were not bothering that snake. Frogs eat mosquitoes and mosquitoes eat me. So I am for letting that frog live and not be et. But a snake would chaw on my leg as quick as he would a frog, so I am for letting a snake die. Anything that bites me must die—snakes, bedbugs, bees, mosquitoes, or bears. I don't even much like for a woman to bite me, though I would not go so far as to kill her. But of all the things that bites, two is worst—a mad dog and a snake. But I would take the dog. I never could understand how in the Bible Eve got near enough to a snake to take an apple."

"Snakes did not bite in those days," I said. "That was the Age of Innocence."

"It was only after Eve got hold of the apple that everything got wrong, huh? Snakes started to bite, women to fight, men to paying, and Christians to praying," said Simple. "It were awful after Eve approached that snake and accepted that apple! It takes a woman to do a fool thing like that."

"Adam ate it, too, didn't he?"

"A woman can make a fool out of a man," said Simple. "But don't let's start talking about women. We have talked about enough unpleasant things for one night. Will you kindly invite me into the bar to have a beer? This sidewalk is hot to my feet. And as a thank-you for a drink, the next time I write a poem, I will give you a copy. But it won't be about the country, neither about nature."

"As much beer as you drink, it will probably be about a bar," I said. "When are you going to wake up, fellow, get wise to yourself, settle down, marry Joyce, and stop gallivanting all over Harlem every night? You're old enough to know better."

"I might be old enough to know better, but I am not old enough to *do* better," said Simple. "Come on in the bar and I will say you a toast I made up the last time somebody told me just what you are saying now about doing better. . . . That's right, bartender, two beers for two steers. . . . Thank you! . . . Pay for them, chum! . . . Now, here goes. Listen fluently:

> *When I get to be ninety-one*
> *And my running days is done,*
> *Then I will do better.*
>
> *When I get to be ninety-two*
> *And just CAN'T do,*
> *I'll do better.*
>
> *When I get to be ninety-three*
> *If the womens don't love me,*
> *Then I must do better.*

When I get to be ninety-four
And can't jive no more,
I'll have to do better.

When I get to be ninety-five,
More dead than alive,
It'll be necessary to do better.

When I get to be ninety-six
And don't know no more tricks,
I reckon I'll do better.

When I get to be ninety-seven
And on my way to Heaven,
I'll try and do better.

When I get to be ninety-eight
And see Saint Peter at the gate,
I know I'll do better.

When I get to be ninety-nine,
Remembering it were fine,
Then I'll do better.

But even when I'm a hundred and one,
If I'm still having fun,
I'll start all over again
Just like I begun—
Because what could be better?"

10

Summer Ain't Simple

"It's summer time," said Simple late one Saturday evening, "but the living ain't easy—no raise in wages and everything still sky-high. Also Joyce mad. I tell you, it ain't easy."

"What's Joyce mad about?"

"Because I don't keep my eyes on her. I was walking down the street with that woman the other night and I just *had* to look back two or three times at what went by. One chick was long, tall, looked like a million dollars—chocolate, man! Another one was high yellow and mellow with her hair blowing back over her ears and her toes sticking out of her shoes pink as the inside of a sugar melon. Man, I could not prevent myself from turning around. Joyce snaps, 'I hate to walk down the street with a man that is always embarrassing me.'

"I said, 'Baby, why is it you do not put pink polish on your toenails, too?'

"Joyce said, 'You are not looking at no toenails. You are looking at limbs.'

"I said, 'If you mean *legs*, baby, I did kinder pass inspection.'

"'You uncouth men embarrass me,' said Joyce. 'If I

wasn't almost home, I would not walk another step with you. I know you want to stop in Paddy's Bar, anyhow. I never did go in the back room of a bar until I started going with you, Jess Semple.' Getting all formal now. 'I do not want to go in a bar tonight. I want me some ice cream to take home.'

"So I had to buy Joyce some ice cream—all because she was mad. I also had to buy enough for her landlady and her landlady's sister—which meant a whole quart. Boy, it takes money to live in the summer time! All the up-town movies are too hot, so she has to go to a downtown movie what's air-cooled. Half a day's pay gone right there. And when she gets home, her room is too stuffy, so she keeps hinting she wishes somebody would buy her a little electric fan.

" 'It seems funny,' Joyce says, 'nobody ever thinks of giving nobody nothing 'less'n it's Christmas.'

"Aw, man, I'm telling you, summer can really become a drag. I am off Saturdays and Sundays, July and August, whilst Joyce is only off Sundays. But I dare not go to no beach on Saturday without her because she will swear I am laying out there in the sun with some other girl—which I am."

"How does Joyce know you have been to the beach un-less you tell her?" I asked.

"I tans quickly. Also, it's hard to get all that sand out of my hair. Joyce can always tell when I have been on the beach."

"But how can she tell you've been with somebody else?"

"I reckon she can see it in my eyes," said Simple. "But a woman ought to know summer ain't no time for a man to keep his eyes on nobody *but* her—with all these fine chicks walking around in frilly dresses and nothing much on underneath."

"Doesn't Joyce dress rather diaphanously?"

"Joyce better not dress like that and let me catch her! You think I want her sashaying up and down the street for every man to whistle at with the sun shining through her skirt like Zarita? Joyce better wear a petticoat."

"You're certainly old-fashioned," I said.

"I may be old-fashioned, but I know what I like."

"In somebody else, yes. You just said you can't keep your eyes off those other girls, which is why you can't keep your eyes *on* Joyce."

"There're times when any man's mind wanders. I'm telling you, it's hard to do right in July. And when comes August, I ain't gonna have a penny saved up for my vacation. I'm gonna have to borrow from Joyce. My papa warn't rich nor my mama good-looking. It's summer time, but the living ain't easy! Facts is, I do not know where I'm going to eat my Sunday dinner. I hate to have my week ends spoiled."

"What do you mean, spoiled?"

"That Joyce has gone over to Jersey to spend Sunday with her foster aunt's cousin's niece whose baby is being christened and Joyce is going to be its godmama. They ask me did I want to be the godpapa, but I said, 'Naw!,' which sounded kinder short-answered. So I thought I better say something nice. So I told 'em, 'As pretty as that little girl is, it will take a better godpapa than me to keep her straight when she grows up. Mens will be running after her like cats after catnip. You pick out some better man for her godpapa.' The way Joyce batted her eyes, I must not of said the right thing. Anyhow, Joyce has gone to Jersey for the cermonials and I have to eat out tomorrow."

"What is so bad about that?"

Simple looked at me in amazement.

"Ain't you ever et in a Harlem restaurant?"

"Certainly, at Bell's or Mrs. Frazier's or Frank's."

"I am not talking about them high-toned places," said Simple, "where they take your week's salary. I am talking about just a plain ordinary restaurant where they wipe the counter off with a dishrag, and where most people eat at."

"I have eaten in such restaurants," I said.

"Then you ought to know what I'm talking about. I went in a nice cheap-looking little place on Seventh Avenue this noon time thinking I would have me a good breakfast. The waitress frowns like I was in the wrong place and comes up and says, 'What do you want?' as if the joint wasn't public.

"I says, 'Gimme some ham and eggs, baby, please.'

"She says, 'Breakfast is *been* over!'

"I says, 'I cannot get no ham and eggs?'

"She says, 'The cook ain't bothering with no breakfast orders now, I told you. It's after noon.'

"I said, 'You ain't told me nothing like that. Anyhow, what have you got for lunch?'

"She puts down an old beat-up menu. I say, 'Gimme side pork and cabbage.'

"She says, 'We don't have that.'

"I say, 'It is writ on here.'

"She says, 'We generally has that on Thursdays and we do not have it today.'

" 'What can I get then for lunch,' I says, 'that you have got?'

" 'Pork chops, fried liver, pot roast, and hog maw,' she says.

"I said, 'Gimme some pot roast.'

"She goes off and in about ten minutes she comes back and says, 'The pot roast ain't ready yet.'

" 'Then gimme the hog maw,' I says, 'because I do not like a lot of fried stuff in the summer.'

" 'The hog maw ain't quite done.'

" 'I can't get breakfast, neither can I get lunch! What have you got?' I says.

" 'I can give you pork chops, fried liver . . .'

" 'You can't give me nothing,' I remarks and walks out. I tried another place further down the street around the corner. Two large fat ladies was sitting on their haunches behind the counter. I sets, but neither one of 'em moves.

"Finally one says, 'You wait on him, Essie. I waited on the last customer.'

"The other one says, 'Aw, go see what that man wants, sis! I'm tired.'

"I said, 'Don't none of you-all move. I will move.' So I moved out.

"I went into a big place on 125th Street. A fine Creole-looking old gal come up and put down a glass of water and a menu card. I hadn't hardly got the card in my hand when she says, 'Make up your mind, daddy. I ain't got all day to stand here.'

" 'Don't stand then,' I said. 'Set down! I'm gone!'

"So I took the subway like I had some sense and went downtown on Broadway where at least you can get some polite service at the Automat. What do you suppose makes them act that way in Harlem restaurants? They look like they are mad when you come in, then they bark at you like a dog, and do not have half of the things they put on the menu. Now, why is that?"

"No doubt because most of them are poor restaurants with untrained personnel."

"Person—hell!" said Simple.

11

A Word from "Town & Country"

"Have you seen Watermelon Joe?" asked Simple, looking around the bar.

"No, I have not," I said. "Why?"

"He owes me a quarter."

"Do you expect to get it back?"

"No."

"Then why did you lend it to him?" I asked.

"From some people you expect to get nothing back," explained Simple, "but you does for them right on."

"Why?" I pursued the question.

"Why do you do for a dog? Why do you do for a woman?"

"Surely you do not put women and dogs in the same class?" I asked.

"Sometimes both of them are b—," Simple began.

"Shsss-ss-s! That is not a polite word," I said. "It will get you in the doghouse with the ladies, and there are ladies in this bar."

"The word for a lady dog *is* a polite word," Simple said. "I have seen it in *Town & Country*, which my boss's wife reads."

"Harlem does not read *Town & Country*," I said. "Colored people think *bitch* is a bad word, not a female hound."

"But I were using it in its good way to mean a woman and a hound," said Simple.

"In polite company, you do not use it for a female unless you mean it to be a hound," I said.

"I do not mean it to be a hound now," said Simple. "I mean it to be a woman who acts like a hound."

"Then you are using it in its profane sense," I said, "and you are insulting womankind."

"My mother was a woman," said Simple indignantly, "and I would not insult her."

"But you would insult *my* mother," I said, "if you applied that term to womankind."

"I do not even know your mother," said Simple.

"Well, I would appreciate it if you did not talk about her now," I said, "in the same breath with female hounds."

"You must be drunk," said Simple. "I did not mention your mother."

"You just got through mentioning my mother," I said, "so how can you say that?"

"I did not say she was that word I saw in *Town & Country*," said Simple.

"You'd better not." I said.

"But women in general are," said Simple.

"My mother is a woman."

"I mean, not including *your mother and mine*," said Simple.

"You're still making it rather broad," I said. "I also know some other women whom I highly respect."

"I will leave them out," said Simple. "But you know

what I mean. Women is women. When you do for them, it is just about the same as doing for Watermelon Joe. You do not expect to get anything back."

"What do you want back?" I asked. "The little bit of money you spend?"

"No," said Simple. "I want love, respect, attention, 'Here is your slippers, daddy,' when I come home. Not, 'Where is that pound of butter I told you to bring?' And I say, 'Aw, woman, I just forgot.' Then she says, 'It is funny you can remember your Cousin Josephine's birthday and send her a card which costs a quarter and you cannot remember to get a pound of butter for your own home. No, you neglect what is nearest to you. I am your wife! Remember?'

"Then I say, 'Of course, you are my wife, Isabel, and I did not forget you. I just forgot the butter. Do you want to make something out of it?'

" 'Yes,' she says, 'I want to make something out of it. You don't work no harder than me and yet you expects me to do the shopping, cooking, cleaning, and wash your filthy clothes, too, when I come home. Yes, I think you should remember that butter! You getting ready to go down to that old bar right now and eyeball them loose womens.' Only she didn't say *womens*. She said that word that was in *Town & Country*. And all I could think of to say back, 'It's a lie! You are the only (word that's in *Town & Country*) that I have gazed at all day—and you hurt my eyes.'

"Then it were on! That is why we did not stay together. A woman is evil. And when a man is tired, sometimes the only word he can think of to say is the one that white

folks use for dogs. I don't know why we can't use it, too."
"Because it is disrespectful to women," I said, "that is why."
"But that is what they is," said Simple.
"Be careful! My mother is a woman," I said.
"I am *not* talking about *your* mother, neither about *my* mother," said Simple. "I am just talking about women."
"Your mother was not a man, was she?"
"I do not play the dozens when I am drinking," said Simple.

12

Matter for a Book

"I saw Jackie yesterday," said Simple as blue Monday drew to a close.

"What Jackie?" I asked, feigning ignorance.

"There ain't but one," said Simple.

"How was he doing?"

"Making home runs and hitting all balls."

"Jackie does not *always* hit," I said.

"I did not see him miss," said Simple.

"You are a Negrophile," I said.

"A which?" said Simple.

"Too much of a race man."

"That's a lie," said Simple. "When my race does wrong, I say, NO. But when they do right, I give 'em credit."

"Credit in moderation is O.K. But overenthusiasm is as bad as not enough. Jackie Robinson is a good ball-player—but there are other good ballplayers on the Dodgers, too."

"None as dark as Jackie," said Simple. "That is why I like him. He is two shades darker than me! Nobody can say he is a Cuban or some kind of foreigner. He is pure-D Negro—and I am proud of it."

"I am proud, too," I said. "But you are mistaken as to

his complexion—Jackie Robinson is not as dark as you. You are what I would call a very dark brownskin."

"I am a light black," said Simple. "When I were a child, Mama said I were chocolate, also my hair was straight. But that was my Indian blood."

"They say folks grow darker as they get older," I said.

"Then there would be no way for age to show on me any more," said Simple. "But to get back to Jackie—I did not mean to holler so loud when he stole them two bases yesterday, but I just could not help myself. I were so proud he were black, I couldn't keep my mouth shut. And as long as Jackie stays colored, I am going to holler when he's up at bat."

"Well, holler. Nobody is stopping you," I said. "But if Jackie were not good you would stop hollering. I bet you that."

"I holler because I am a race man," said Simple.

"In other words, you are cheering yourself then," I said.

"And anybody connected with me! I want my race to hit home all the time."

"That's a very laudable desire," I said. "And I hope you are doing your part to help your race go on, up, and ever forward. I trust you are trying just as hard as Jackie."

"I am," said Simple. "I'm *cheering*."

"Figures in the sports field like Jackie and Joe rate plenty of cheering. But sometimes I wish the public were equally aware of the men of our race in the cultural fields. You, for instance, have you ever bought a book by a Negro writer?"

"Joyce is the one who likes to read," said Simple. "That

girl reads a book a week, sometimes two—and I don't mean comic books neither. I don't go in for reading much myself, but Joyce is cultural. The other night when I stopped by, she was reading a book about some vixens and—"

"Frank Yerby's *The Vixens,* I guess."

"That were it," said Simple. "Man, that story is real gone! Joyce says a colored man wrote it."

"That's right, Frank Yerby is colored."

"And Joyce says he wrote a book before that about the wolves of Harlem," continued Simple.

"What she probably said was not *wolves* at all. You have your animals and places mixed up. His first best seller was *The Foxes of Harrow,* not *The Wolves of Harlem.*"

"Say not so," said Simple. "It is good when a colored man writes a book."

"Not necessarily," I said. "Colored books can be bad, too. But it just happens that both of Yerby's books were best sellers, and they made a movie of *The Foxes of Harrow.*"

"That is real great," said Simple.

"In fact, we've had other books by Negroes on the best-seller list, among them, Richard Wright's *Black Boy* and Willard Motley's *Knock on Any Door.* The race is rising," I said.

"All but me," said Simple. "I ain't got nowhere and I'm colored. In fact, of late I have gone back. My finances have been cut and my wages are lower while everything else is higher. My landlady is mad because she can't get a raise in rent so the hot water is cold and she put a ten-watt bulb in the bathroom so I can't even see to shave. This morning I paid seventy cents for two little old dried-up slivers of bacon and one cockeyed egg. It took me till noon to get my appetite back. Then it cost me a dollar for lunch. If I hadn't et dinner with Joyce this evening I would have been tee-totally broke."

"It is not food alone that keeps you broke," I said pointedly.

"If you mean licker, I am not able to hardly drink more than a drop. I am not Jackie Robinson—up in the money. But say, since that writer fellow made all that money out of *The Foxes of Harry,* maybe I could write *me* a book and call it *The Wolves of Harlem* by Jesse Semple."

"What would you put in your book?"

"Chapter Number One. I would start out on Lenox Avenue. Then I would bring in the wolves. I would show how if prices keep high as they is and wages go down, not a living wolf will be able to howl this time next year. They can do no more than go to work and come back weak, man, weak."

"What will you put in Chapter Two?" I asked.

"That will be a killer," said Simple. "In Chapter Number Two, I will put the plot."

"What is the plot?"

"That I will not tell," said Simple, "you are liable to steal it."

"What is your love interest, then? Your romance? In a novel you have to have romance."

"Who has got time for romance, as high as meat stays?" objected Simple. "Romance costs money. I will not put no romance in my book. I will put beefsteaks, pork chops, spare ribs, pigs' feet, and ham in *my* story."

"Then-all your hero will do is eat like a wolf," I said, "which is not very edifying."

"*Satisfying,* though," said Simple.

13

Surprise

"There are lots of curs in the human race," said Simple. "Some very sweet—but curs right on."

"Referring, for example, to what?" I asked.

"To women right now," said Simple, "for example, Vivian."

"She did do Johnny rather badly, didn't she?"

"Moved out, left him, and didn't even leave him a note," said Simple. "And he had been taking care of her like a queen all these years. He hadn't no more than been out of work two weeks till she was up and gone with another huck. Women cannot stand for a man to get out of work. My wife was like that."

"Love and hunger do not mix," I said, "except in books, where, of course, people are faithful until death, job or no job."

"Books have nothing to do with life," said Simple; "they are like movies. In movies gangsters always come to a bad ending. In life, they live on Park Avenue and eat at the Waldorf. But you are changing my subject. I am talking about curs, not books. Did you hear what that sweet little cur-hussy of a Lauretta did to Rudolph?"

"Rudolph? I thought he was in the army."

"He come back from occupying Japan this morning and is occupying a jail tonight," said Simple.

"No!"

"Yes, he is. And he had not been home in three years. His mistake was not to let his wife know he was coming. A soldier should always let his old lady know when he plans to return to the fold."

"He no doubt wished to surprise her," I said.

"He surprised his own self," said Simple. "Order me another beer so I can tell you what happened as Zarita told it to me. Fellow, it were awful!"

"Give the man a beer," I said. "Now, go on."

"A week end is the wrong time to come home anyhow," said Simple. "So many people do not work on Saturdays nowadays. Lucky it were not me! I tried to make time with Lauretta myself while Rudolph were in Tokyo, but she liked that old conk-headed boy that works in the dye plant—you know, light black Freddy. You saw them both in here last night drinking Scotch. Well, seems like yesterday being Friday and Freddy did not have to work no more till Monday, he went home with Lauretta and were laying up there in her apartment this morning when Rudolph got in."

"No!" I said.

"Yes, he were," said Simple. "Rudolph took a taxi from the station because he had too many Japanese swords, Chinese gongs, and Hawaiian grass skirts to come in the subway—all of which he bought for presents for his wife. He got to Harlem about ten A.M. Seems like Lauretta had gone to the A & P store to purchase some grits. Before she left out, she told Freddy, 'Honey, just you stay in bed till I get back and I will squeeze you some nice fresh orange juice. You hear, Freddy, honey? Then you can bathe yourself while I fix breakfast.'

"Freddy said, 'Ummm-mm-hum!' and turned over to sleep some more.

"Whilst Lauretta were gone, Rudolph arrived on his furlough, put his key in the lock, and started to set his stuff down in the hall. Well, sir, Freddy heard them grass skirts rustling and he thought it were Lauretta with her paper bags from the store. So he calls out, 'Baby, bring me a nice cooo-oo-o-ool glass of water before you squeeze that orange juice.'

"What did Freddy say that for—and her husband right there in the hall? Rudolph sweated blood, also tears. But he did not say a thing. He just eased his pistol out of his bag, tiptoed into his bedroom, aimed that gun at his bed, and said, 'Who wants a nice cooo-oo-o-ool glass of water, huh?'

"Freddy were too petrified to reply when he noticed it were Lauretta's husband. In fact, he were speechless. Rudolph made him get up out of *his* bed, take off *his* pajamas, and jump buck naked in the closet, where he locked him up. Then Rudolph himself put them pajamas on—after hiding his grass skirts and his gear so Lauretta would not see. Then he got in his *own* bed for the first time in three years and turned his back like as if he were asleep. In a few minutes the hall door opened and in come Lauretta.

" 'Freddy, baby,' she called, 'wake up now. I'll have your orange juice in a minute, darling.'

" 'Um-m-hum-m-m . . . ,' said Rudolph, pretending to be Freddy half asleep.

"It were a long minute to him, I reckon. And even longer to Freddy, locked in that closet. But finally Lauretta came from the kitchen with the orange juice, ice just a-tinkling. Rudolph had his back turned and his arm stretched out in them same striped pajamas as Freddy had had on.

" 'Wake up, Freddy, baby, and turn over and drink this nice cold juice,' Lauretta said. When he did not move, Lauretta shook his shoulder in the bed very sweet-like. 'Wake up, honey, here!'

"Honey turned—but it were not the man she had left there a-tall! Not Freddy—but her husband!

"I cannot tell you what happened to Lauretta—except that the least she did was to faint. And the orange juice spoiled her counterpane. Rudolph were too much of a gentleman to shoot her. But he whipped her with everything at hand, including a grass skirt. He did not kill Freddy neither. But Freddy will not go to the dye works for some time because both of his eyes is closed. And Rudolph is in jail the first day he come back home.

"Zarita says she told Lauretta to bathe her face in witch hazel to take the bruises off. I hope that helps because Lauretta is a right sweet girl, even if she did act like a little old cur-fice dog while Rudolph was in Tokyo. But Rudolph really ought to of let her know he was coming home. A surprise like that is not pleasant for all concerned."

14

Vacation

"What's on the rail for the lizard this morning?" my friend Simple demanded about 1 A.M. at 125th and Lenox.

"Where have you been all week?" I countered, looking at the dark circles under his eyes.

"On my vacation *at last,*" said Simple.

"You look it! You appear utterly fatigued."

"A vacation will tire a man out worse than work," said Simple.

"Where did you go?"

"Saratoga—after the season was over and the rates is down."

"What did you do up there?"

"Got bug-eyed."

"You mean drank liquor?" I inquired.

"I did not drink water," said Simple.

"I thought people went to Saratoga Springs to drink water."

"Some do, some don't," said Simple, "depending on if you are thirsty or not. There is no water on Congress Street, nothing but bars—Jimmie's, Goldie's, Hilltop House. Man, I had myself a ball. I was wild and frantic as a Halloween pumpkin, drinking cool keggie and knock-

ing myself out. I met some fine chicks, too! The first night
I was there one big fat mellow dame, looking all sweet
and sweetened, started making admiration over me. I
would not tell you a word of lie, she wanted to latch on
to me for life."

"Where was Joyce?"

"You know I did not take Joyce with me on no vacation," said Simple. "I left her in Harlem. Her vacation
and mine does not come at the same time anyhow, and
we do not go the same places. Joyce is a quiet girl. But
this old girl I met in Saratoga—oh, boy! We was sitting
at the bar. She started jitterbugging right on the stool,
so I introduced myself. She said, 'Baby, play that piece
again,' which I did. Then she said, 'Play "The Huckle-
buck" about six times,' which I also did."

"So that's where your money went," I said, "right over
the bar and down the juke box?"

"That's where it went," said Simple, "but it were worth
it. This old gal looked like chocolate icing on a wagon-
wheel cake, partner. And I met another one looked like
lemon meringue on a Sunday pie. Between the two of
them I had a ball! But I come back to Harlem a week
early because my money ran out. When I got home, first
thing I did was go see Joyce.

"She said, 'Baby, how come you back so soon?'

"I said, 'Sugar, I wanted to see you'—and don't you
know, Joyce believed me! Womens is simple.

"Joyce said, 'You sure do look tired.'

"I said, 'It's from just a-wearying for you, honey. I
can't stay away from you a week at a time no more without it worries me.'

"Joyce said, 'I thought you would come back here looking all spruce and spry from drinking that sulphur water,
baby.'

"But I told her, 'That water did not agree with me.
Neither did that Saratoga food. Honey, you know the best
thing about a vacation is coming home. When are you
going to make some biscuits?'

"Man, don't you know Joyce went right out in the
kitchen and made me some bread! I was hongry, too.
Funny how fast your money can run out on a vacation."

"Especially when you're spending it on *two* women," I
said. "You have got to learn to change your character and
budget *both* your money and your pleasure."

"God gave me this character," said Simple. "In His
own good time He will change it. You know that old
saying:

> *A bobtail dog*
> *Can't walk a log.*
> *Neither can a elephant*
> *Hop like a frog.*

My character is *my* character! It cannot change."

"It's certainly true that nobody can make a silk purse
out of a sow's ear," I said.

"Who wants to?" asked Simple.

PART TWO

Winter Time

15

Letting Off Steam

"Winter time in Harlem sure is a blip," Simple complained. "I have already drunk four beers and one whiskey and I am not warm yet."

"Your blood must be thin," I said.

"Thin, nothing! It's just cold out there. I do not like cold, never did, and never will, no place, no time."

"Well, what are you doing out in this weather if you're so cold-natured? Why didn't you stay home?"

"Man, this bar is the warmest place I know. At least they keep the steam up here."

"You mean to tell me you haven't got any steam in your room?"

"There's a radiator in my room," said Simple, "but my landlady don't send up no steam. I beat on the radiator pipes to let her know I was home—and freezing."

"What happened?"

"Nothing. She just beat back on the pipes at me! I tell you, winter is a worriation."

"I don't like the cold, either," I said. "But mortal man can do very little about the weather. Of course, one could be rich and go to Florida."

"You couldn't give me Florida and all that Jim Crow

on a silver platter! But if these womens keep after me, I am liable to have to go somewhere."

"What's the matter now?" I asked.

"My wife writ me from Baltimore that if I don't buy her that divorce she's been wanting for seven years, she is going to get herself a new fur coat and charge it to me. She says I better pay for it or else! And Joyce has been hinting around lately that she needs a silver fox—and she ain't even married to me yet. Here I am going around wearing my prewar Chesterfield and can't get a new coat for myself. I ain't even got no rubbers for this snow."

"You love Joyce, don't you? So I know you wouldn't want to see her freeze."

"Freeze, nothing," said Simple. "If Joyce would put on some long underwear and drop them skirts down some more and wrap up her neck, she would be warm without a fur coat. Also, if she would stop wearing open-worked shoes. Women don't wear enough clothes."

"Do you want your best girl to look like somebody's grandma?"

"I don't want her to catch pneumonia," said Simple, "but I *ain't* gonna buy her no fur coat."

"A fur coat would have made a nice gift for Christmas. By the way, what did you give Joyce?"

"A genuine pressure-cooker-roasting-oven to cook chickens, since I like them. It cost me fifteen dollars, too. But when I was back in the kitchen Christmas Eve mixing drinks she came in and gave me one of them cold-roll-your-eyes looks and said real sweet-like, 'It's just what I wanted—except that I've got too many cooking utensils now to be just rooming—and that cute little fur jacket I showed you last week would've looked so nice on me.' "

"What did Joyce give you for Christmas?" I asked.

"A carton of *her* favorite brand of cigarettes. Ain't that just like a woman? Then she comes wanting a fur coat."

"Well, even dogs have fur coats. I see in the papers where a downtown store is advertising fur wrappers especially for dogs, priced up to Two Thousand Dollars. If someone would pay that much for a fur coat for a dog, it looks as though you might consider one for Joyce."

"Man, the rich peoples that buy them expensive dog-jackets have paid Two Thousand Bucks for their dog in the first place. To have a fur coat like that, the dog is bound to be a thoroughbred-pedigreedy-canine dog. They ain't buying fur wrap-arounds for no mutt. They got their investment to protect. But Joyce ain't cost me nothing. Money couldn't buy that girl. I met her on a Negro Actors' Guild public boat ride when the moon were shining over Bear Mountain. She just floated into my life— free. And took up with me for the sake of love."

"So you would value a dog more than the woman who is your friend?"

"I do not have a dog, and if I did, as sure as my name is Jess Semple, I would not buy it no fur coat—a dog has its own fur. And unless Joyce raises herself some foxes, she will not get any, neither. I won't buy a human nor a dog a fur coat this winter."

"Why don't you just say you *can't* buy a fur coat?"

"You have hit the nail on the head. I have just cash enough for *one* more beer. You have that glass on me."

"No, thanks."

"Then I will have a *bottle* on you," said Simple, "before I go out in the cold. The Lord should have fixed it so humans can grow fur in the winter time—instead of buying it. . . . Hey, Bud, a bottle of Bud!"

16

Jealousy

"That Joyce," said Simple, "is not a drinking woman —for which I love her. But if she wasn't my girl friend, I swear she would make me madder than she do sometimes."

"What's come off between you and Joyce now?" I asked.

"She has upset me," said Simple.

"How?"

"One night last week when we come out of the subway, it was sleeting too hard to walk and we could not get a cab for love nor money. So Joyce condescends to stop in the Whistle and Rest with me and have a beer. If I had known what was in there, I would of kept on to Paddy's, where they don't have nothing but a juke box."

"What was in there?"

"A trio," said Simple. "They was humming and strumming up a breeze with the bass just a-thumping, piano trilling, and electric guitar vibrating with every string overcharged. They was playing off-bop. Now, I do not care much for music, and Joyce does not care much for beer. So after I had done had from four to six and she had had two, I said, 'Let's go.' Joyce said, 'No, baby! I want to stay awhile more.'

"Now that were the first time I have ever heard Joyce say she wants to set in a bar.

"I said, 'What ails you?'

"Joyce said, 'I *love* his piano playing.'

"I said, 'You sure it ain't the piano *player* you love?' He were a slickheaded cat that looked like a shmoo and had a part in his teeth.

"Joyce said, 'Don't insinuate.'

"I said, 'Before you sin, *you* better wait. It looks like to me that piano player is eying you mighty hard. He'd best keep his eyes on them keys, else I will close one and black the other, also be-bop his chops.'

"Joyce says, 'Huh! It is about time you got a little jealous of me, Jess. Sometimes I think you take me for granted. But I *do* like that man's music.'

" 'Are you sure it's his music you like?' I says. 'As flirtatious as you is this evening, your middle name ought to be Frisky.'

" 'Don't put me in no class with Zarita,' says Joyce right out of the clear skies. 'I am no bar-stool hussy'—which kinder took me back because I did not know Joyce had any information about Zarita. A man can't do nothing even once without Harlem and his brother knowing it. Somebody has been talking, or else Joyce is getting too well acquainted with some of my friends—like you."

"I never mention your personal affairs to anyone," I said, "least of all to Joyce, whom I scarcely know except through your introduction."

"Well, anyhow," said Simple, "I did not wish to argue. I says to her, 'I ignore that remark.'

"Joyce says, 'I ignore you.' And turned her back to me and cupped her ear to the music.

" 'Don't rile me, woman,' I says. 'Come out of here and lemme take you home. You know we have to work in the morning.'

" 'Work does not cross your mind,' says Joyce, turning around, 'when you're setting up drinking beer all by yourself—so you say—at Paddy's. I do not see why you have to mention work to *me* when I am enjoying *myself*. The way that man plays "Stardust" sends me. I swear it do. Sends me. Sends me!'

" 'Be yourself, Joyce,' I said. 'Put your coat around your shoulders. Are you high? We are going home.'

"I took Joyce out of there. And by Saturday, to tell the truth, I had forgot all about it. Come the weekend, I says, 'Let's walk a little, honey. Which movie do you want to see?'

"Joyce says, 'I do not want to see a picture, daddy. They are all alike. Let's go to the Whistle and Rest Bar.'

" 'O.K.,' I said, because I knowed every Friday they change the music behind that bar. They had done switched to a great big old corn-fed blues man who looked like Ingagi, hollered like a mountain-jack, and almost tore a guitar apart. He were singing:

> *Where you goin', Mr. Spider,*
> *Walking up the wall?*
> *Spider said, I'm goin'*
> *To get my ashes hauled.*

The joint were jumping—rocking, rolling, whooping, hollering, and stomping. It was a far cry from "Stardust" to that spider walking up the wall.

"When I took Joyce in and she did not see her light-dark shmoo with the conked crown curved over the piano smearing riffs, she said, 'Is this the same place we was at last time?'

"I said, 'Sure, baby! What's the matter? Don't you like blues?'

"Joyce said, 'You know I never did like blues. I am from the North.'

" 'North what?' I said. 'Carolina?'

" 'I thought this was a refined cocktail lounge,' says Joyce, turning up her nose. 'But I see I was in error. It's a low dive. Let's go on downtown and catch John Garfield after all.'

" 'No, no, no. No *after all* for me,' I said. 'Here we are —and here we stay right in this bar till *I* get ready to go. . . . Waiter, a beer! . . . Anyhow, I do not see why *you* would want to see John Garfield. Garfield does not conk his hair. Neither is he light black. Neither does he play "Stardust." '

" 'You are acting just like a Negro,' says Joyce.

" 'It's my Indian blood,' I admitted."

17

Banquet in Honor

"Well, sir, I went to a banquet the other night," said Simple, "and I have never seen nothing like it. The chicken was good, but the best thing of all was the speech."

"That's unusual," I said. "Banquet speeches are seldom good."

"This one were a killer," said Simple. "In fact, it almost killed the folks who gave the function."

"Who gave it?"

"Some women's club that a big fat lady what goes to Joyce's dancing class belongs to. Her name is Mrs. Sadie Maxwell-Reeves and she lives so high up on Sugar Hill that people in her neighborhood don't even have roomers. They keep the whole house for themselves. Well, this Mrs. Maxwell-Reeves sold Joyce a deuce of Three-Dollar ducats to this banquet her club was throwing for an old gentleman who is famous around Harlem for being an intellect for years, also very smart as well as honest, and a kind of all-around artist-writer-speaker and what-not. His picture's in the *Amsterdam News* this week. I cannot recall his name, but I never will forget his speech."

"Tell me about it, man, and do not keep me in suspense," I said.

"Well, Joyce says the reason that club gave the banquet is because the poor old soul is so old he is about on his last legs and, although he is great, nobody has paid him much mind in Harlem before. So this club thought instead of having a dance this year they would show some intelligence and honor him. They did. But he bit their hand, although he ate their chicken."

"I beg you, get to the point, please."

"It seems like this old man has always played the race game straight and has never writ no Amos and Andy books nor no songs like "That's Why Darkies Are Born" nor painted no kinky-headed pictures as long as he has been an artist—for which I give him credit. But it also seems like he did not make any money because the white folks wouldn't buy his stuff and the Negroes didn't pay him no mind because he wasn't already famous.

"Anyhow, they say he will be greater when he's dead than he is alive—and he's mighty near dead now. Poor old soul! The club give that banquet to catch some of his glory before he passes on. He gloried them, all right! In the first place, he ate like a horse. I was setting just the third table from him and I could see. Mrs. Maxwell-Reeves sort of likes Joyce because Joyce helps her with her high kicks, so she give us a good table up near the speaking. She knows Joyce is a fiend for culture, too. Facts, some womens—including Joyce—are about culture like I am about beer—they love it.

"Well, when we got almost through with the dessert, which was ice cream, the toastmistress hit on a cup with a spoon and the program was off. Some great big dame

with a high voice and her hands clasped on her bosoms—
which were fine—sung 'O Carry Me Homey.' "

"'O Caro Nome,' " I said.

"Yes," said Simple. "Anyhow, hard as I try, daddy-o,
I really do not like concert singers. They are always singing in some foreign language. I leaned over the table and
asked Joyce what the song meant, but she snaps, 'It is not
important what it means. Just listen to that high C above
X.' I listened fluently, but it was Dutch to me.

"I said, 'Joyce, what *is* she saying?'

"Joyce said, 'Please don't show your ignorance here.'

"I said, 'I am trying to hide it. But what in God's name
is she singing about?'

"Joyce said, 'It's in Italian. Shsss-ss-s! For my sake,
kindly act like you've got some culture, even if you ain't.'

"I said, 'I don't see why culture can't be in English.'

"Joyce said, 'Don't embarrass me. You ought to be
ashamed.'

"I said, 'I am not ashamed, neither am I Italian, and
I do not understand their language.' We would have had
a quarrel right then and there had not that woman got
through and set down. Then a man from the Urban
League, a lady from the Daughter Elks, and a gentleman
librarian all got up and paid tributes to the guest of honor.
And he bowed and smiled and frowned and et because he
could not eat fast, his teeth being about gone, so he still
had a chicken wing in his hand when the program started.
Finally came the great moment.

" 'Shsss-ss-s-ssh!' says Joyce.

" 'I ain't said a word,' I said, 'except that *I sure wish I
could smoke in here.'*

" 'Hush,' says Joyce, 'this is a cultural event and no smoking is allowed. We are going to hear the guest of honor.'

"You should have seen Mrs. Sadie Maxwell-Reeves. She rose to her full heights. She is built like a pyramid upside down anyhow. But her head was all done fresh and shining with a hair-rocker roached up high in front, and a advertised-in-*Ebony* snood down the back, also a small bunch of green feathers behind her ear and genuine diamonds on her hand. Man, she had bosom-glasses that pulled out and snapped back when she read her notes. But she did not need to read no notes, she were so full of her subject.

"If words was flowers and he was dead, that old man could not have had more boquets put on him if he'd had a funeral at Delaney's where big shots get laid out. Roses, jonquils, pea-lilies, forget-me-nots, pansies, dogwoods, African daisies, also hydrangeas fell all over his head out of that lady toastmistress's mouth. He were sprayed with the perfume of eloquence. He were welcomed and rewelcomed to that Three-Dollar Banquet and given the red plush carpet. Before that lady got through, I clean forgot I wanted to smoke. I were spellbound, smothered in it myself.

"Then she said, 'It is my pride, friends, my pleasure, nay, my honor— without further words, allow me to present this distinguished guest, our honoreeeee—the Honorable Dr. So-and-So-and-So.' I did not hear his name for the applause.

"Well, sir! That old man got up and he did not smile. It looked like he cast a wicked eye right on me, and he did like a snake charmer to Joyce, because nobody could move

our heads. He did not even clear his throat before he said,
'You think you are honoring me, ladies and gentlemen of
the Athenyannie Arts Club, when you invited me here
tonight? You are *not* honoring me a damn bit! I said, not
a bit.'

"You could have heard a pin drop. Mens glued to their
seats. Joyce, too.

" 'The way you could have honored me if you had
wanted to, ladies and gentlemen, all these years, would
have been to buy a piece of my music and play it, or a
book of mine and read it, but you didn't. Else you could
have booed off the screen a few of them Uncle Toms
thereon and told the manager of the Hamilton you'd never
come back to see another picture in his theater until he
put a story of mine in it, or some other decent hard-work-
ing Negro. But you didn't do no such a thing. You didn't
even buy one of my watercolors. You let me starve until I
am mighty nigh blue-black in the face—and not a one of
you from Sugar Hill to Central Park ever offered me a
pig's foot. Then when the *New York Times* said I was a
genius last month, here you come now giving a banquet
for me when I'm old enough to fall over in my grave—if
I was able to walk to the edge of it—which I'm not.

" 'Now, to tell you the truth, I don't want no damned
banquet. I don't want no honoring where *you* eat as much
as me, and enjoy yourselves more, besides making some
money for your treasury. If you want to honor me, give
some young boy or girl who's coming along trying to create
arts and write and compose and sing and act and paint and
dance and make something out of the beauties of the
Negro race—give that child some help. Buy what they're

making! Support what they're doing! Put out some cash —but don't come giving me, who's old enough to die and too near blind to create anything any more anyhow, a great big banquet that *you* eat up in honor of your *own* stomachs as much as in honor of me—who's toothless and can't eat. You hear me, I ain't honored!'

"That's what that old man said, and sat down. You could have heard a pin drop if ary one had dropped, but nary one dropped. Well, then Mrs. Maxwell-Reeves got up and tried to calm the waters. But she made matters worse, and that feather behind her ear was shaking like a leaf. She pulled at her glasses but she could not get them on.

"She said, "Doctor, we know you are a great man, but, to tell the truth, we have been kinder vague about just what you have done.'

"The old man said, 'I ain't done nothing but eat at banquets all my life, and I am great just because I am honored by you tonight. Is that clear?'

"The lady said, 'That's beautiful and so gracious. Thanks. It sounds so much like Father Divine.'

"The old man said, 'Father Divine is a genius at saying the unsayable. That is why he is great and because he also gives free potatoes with his gospel—and potatoes are just as important to the spirit as words. In fact, more so. I know.'

" 'Do you really think so, Doctor?'

" 'Indeed, or I wouldn't have come here at all tonight. I ate in spite of the occasion. I still need a potato and some meat—not honor.'

" 'We are proud to give you both,' said Mrs. Sadie Max-well-Reeves.

" 'Compliment returned,' said the old man. 'The tickets you sold to this affair on the strength of *my* name are feeding us all.'

"Mrs. Sadie Maxwell-Reeves came near blushing, but she couldn't quite make it, being brownskin. I don't know what I did, but everybody turned and looked at me.

"I said, 'Joyce, I got to go have a smoke.'

"Joyce said, 'This is so embarrassing! You laughing out loud! Oh!'

"I said, 'It's the best Six Dollars' worth of banquet I ever had.' (Because I paid for them tickets although Joyce bought them.) I said, 'If you ever want to take me to another banquet in honor, I will go, though I don't reckon there will be another one this good.'

" 'You have a low sense of humor, Mr. Semple,' said Joyce, all formal and everything like she does when she's mad. 'Shut up so I can hear the benediction.'

"Reverend Patterson Smythe prayed. Then it were over. I beat it on out of there and had my smoke whilst I was waiting for Joyce, because she looked mad. On the way home I stopped at the Wonder Bar and had two drinks, but Joyce would not even come in the back room. She waited in the cab. She said I were not the least bit cultural. Still and yet, I thought that old man made sense. I told Joyce, just like he said, 'It is more important to eat than to be honored, ain't it?'

"Joyce said, 'Yes, but when you are doing both at the same time, you can at least be polite. I mean not only the Doctor, but *you*. It's an honor to be invited to things like that. And Mrs. Maxwell-Reeves did not invite you there to laugh.'

"I said, 'I didn't know I was laughing.'

" 'Everybody else knew it,' she said when we got to her door. 'You was heard all over the hall. I was embarrassed not only for you, *but for myself.* I would like you to know that I am not built like you. I cannot just drink and forget.'

" 'No matter how many drinks I drink,' I said, 'I will not forget this.' Then I laughed again—which were my error! I did not even get a good-night kiss—Joyce slammed the vestibule door dead in my face. So I went home to my Third Floor Rear—*and laughed some more.* If I wasn't honored, I sure was tickled, and, at least, I ain't stingy like them Sugar-Hillers. They wouldn't buy none of his art when he could still enjoy the benefits. But me, I'd buy that old man a beer *any time.*"

18

After Hours

"Bartender!" Simple cried in a loud voice as though he were going to treat everyone in the place. "Once around the bar." Then pointing to ourselves, "This far—from my buddy to me."

By the time the beers were drawn, Simple had begun to recount a story.

"You know," he began, "I was way down under in Harlem the other night, way, way down on Lenox Avenue." I could see it was a serious story because he forgot his beer, allowing his glass to remain on the bar.

"It was so cold I went into a barbecue place thinking I might take a order of spareribs and coleslaw to Joyce if I had enough change—and at the same time get warm. Man, the juke box was playing up a breeze, flashing colored lights, and the joint was full of young kids and girls not buying nothing much but drinking Pepsis and jiving around the juke box. I looked at them kids and I felt sorry. I can see now why these girls wear open-worked shoes in zero weather because them cheap soles are so thin they couldn't keep their feet warm anyhow, so they'd just as well be open-worked.

"And the boys," continued Simple, "with them army-

store raincoats on and last spring's imitation camel's hairs
—which would not keep nobody warm—because they ain't
had the money this winter to buy an overcoat. They was
just jiving and jitterbugging quietly-like, till the woman
hollered, 'Stop!' because there was a big sign up:

NO DANCING POSITIVELY

"They also had a sign up:

DON'T ASK FOR CREDIT—HE'S DEAD

"I reckon that is why those kids could not eat much, on
account of credit being dead. But they had to move to keep
warm because it was kinder cold in that place, the only
heat being from that thing where the barbecue turns and
that was not much. It were a Greek place or some kind
of foreigner's, but at least they had colored help. The
foreigner just set behind the cash register and took the
money.

"While I was setting there waiting for the woman to
wrap up my sandwich and coleslaw for Joyce, a half-dozen
little old teen-age boys come in and stood around listening
to the juke box, singing with the records and rubbing their
ears to get warm. By and by a quarrel started amongst
them and before you could say 'Hush,' one of them let a
blackjack a foot long slide out of his sleeve and another
one drew a knife. They all started cussing and damning.

"The woman behind the counter said, 'Somebody ought
to call the Law,' which kinder riled me the wrong way
because after all, they was nothing but kids.

"So I said, 'Madam, the cops could only lock them kids
up. The cops could not make their papa's kitchenette big
enough for them to invite their young friends to come

home and have fun in and not have to look for it in the
streets. I bet where these boys live there are forty-eleven
names in the doorbell, the house is so crowded. Also some
roomer has the spare bed.'

"The woman said, 'I reckon you right. There are about
that many names in the bell where I live, too. But I just
don't want these boys to fight in here, that's all. They make
me nervous.'

"The boys didn't fight. They finally put up their weap-
ons, and I took my sandwich and coleslaw and went on up
the street. Zero outside, man! And cold enough to freeze
a brass monkey! But all the way to Joyce's I kept thinking
about them kids that didn't have no place to go in the
evening but to that juke-box joint with a sign up:

NO DANCING POSITIVELY

"I said to myself, 'If I ever have a kid, I will have a juke
box *at home* and his friends can come in and dance as
much as they want.' "

"A victrola would be more appropriate for the home,"
I said.

"A juke box is more sociable," declared Simple, "then
they wouldn't get into the habit of wanting to be out in
the streets so much and later when they got grown start
to running around to bars and after-hour joints."

"Like you," I said.

"Yes, like me," said Simple. "I almost got caught in a
raid the other night. But the cops phoned first that they
was coming. The raid were just a polite hint to the house-
man to keep their graft up to date and let the Law have
theirs on time. I guess the reason cops are so hard on after-

first thing she asked me? She said, 'Where was you the night before?'

"I said, 'I was out, baby, in an after-hours place, and I did not get home till late.'

"She said, 'That is no excuse for you to come around to my house and set up and snooze. I do not pay rent here to receive sleepers. Suppose my landlady was to walk in and catch you sleeping in her parlor.'

"I said, 'So what? When a man is tired, he has to sleep. Besides, I got a headache.'

"She said, 'A licker-ache, that's what! I can smell wood alcohol from your end of the couch to mine. Get out of here and go on home. You ain't no company to me in your condition.'

"Joyce were mad! That is why I am not keeping her company this evening. And that is what I am telling you about a woman not understanding a man. The very time you need to be understood most is the time they let you down. Hang-overed as I was, Joyce should have said, 'Baby, lemme put a cold towel on your head.' Instead of that, she said, 'Get out of here and go home! You ain't no company for me.' Now, if Joyce had come to see me feeling bad, I would have tried to comfort her."

"You would not be going with Joyce if she were the kind of girl who gets drunk and has hang-overs," I said.

"True," answered Simple.

"Then why do you expect her to understand you when you come up in that condition?"

"*Because I am a man*," said Simple, "and a woman is suppose to understand. There is nothing worse than a hang-over. So if *ever* there is a time to understand, that time is it. I am disappointed in Joyce."

"Joyce is probably disappointed in you," I said, "spending your money collecting hang-overs in joints like Mojo Mike's after hours."

"After hours is when I needs most to be understood," said Simple, "especially *after* after hours."

women started yapping at each other all over again. Man, a woman is something!

" 'I'll get a cab,' the tall one yells.

" 'I'll get it and pay for it, too,' hollered the little one. 'I know Charlie snuck off from me to go see you today. But I'm the one he comes to first—like this afternoon—first—soon as he gets in town.'

" 'That's what you think,' says the tall woman. 'Wheee-eeooo! Cab!'

" 'I'm the one he gets a dollar from when he needs it most,' yaps the little chick. 'Long as I'm working, Charlie'll eat! I'll get this cab and pay for it. Do you hear me, Cassie?'

"Some old agitating Negro standing in the doorway of the bar yells, 'One of you women better hurry up and get that taxi or won't neither one of you-all have no man. He'll be gone.'

"The soldier-boy did start to walk, but that leg—he must of hurt them nerve ends when he fell. I imagine it was like a aching tooth and he couldn't keep from grabbing it. Leaning on them crutches trying to keep his hands from going to that sawed-off leg, but he couldn't keep from grabbing it. He just stood still. I didn't know what to say to him, so I thought I would take my handkerchief and wipe some of the wet off the back of his coat.

"But he said, 'Get away, man!'

"It was old Dad Martin what owns that little hamburger stand that did the best thing. Dad come out and said, 'Son, anybody could fall down on this wet night. Is you hurt?'

" 'Naw, Dad, I just slipped, that's all.'

" 'I mean, did it hurt your feelings?' Dad said.

" 'No,' said the soldier.

" 'Then everything's all right,' the old man said.

"Just then Cassie hollered, 'Baby, here's the cab! Come on!'

"The little woman beat Cassie to him, though. 'Here's our taxi, honey! Come on, Charlie, we got a cab.'

" 'You better set between them two women else they liable to tear each other's eyes out,' yells that agitating old Negro in the bar door.

" 'Everything's under control,' said the soldier, 'don't worry.'

"He pulled his own self up in that cab. But the women jumped in after him and there he was between them when the taxi pulled off in the rain—and they was still fussing over who he belonged to. It was funny—still and yet it wasn't funny either.

"You can laugh at a man when he falls if he's got two legs, but I couldn't laugh at him. Couldn't nobody laugh at that soldier like they would laugh at you and me if we fell down trying to ignore a couple of women. That's why it was kinder hard for that boy to take. I aimed to order a beer when I got in the bar but my mouth said, 'A double whiskey!' It damn sure did, after that boy fell down."

20

High Bed

"I told you you should take care of yourself," I said to Simple as I sat down beside his bed. "Running around half high in all this cold weather. If you had taken care of yourself, and not gotten all run down, you would not be here now in this hospital with pneumonia."

"If I had taken care of myself," said Simple, "I would not have these pretty nurses taking care of me."

"Everything has its compensations, I admit. But look at the big hospital bill you will have when you get out."

"Just let me draw two or three weeks' pay or hit one number, and I will settle it," said Simple. "But what worries me is when am I going to get out?"

"You should have worried about that before you got in," I said. "And you will never get out if you do not observe the rules and stop telling folks to bring you beer and pigs' feet and things you are not supposed to have."

"You didn't bring me that Three Feathers I told you to bring," said Simple. "And the nurse would not let me finish that little old sausage Zarita brought in her pocketbook yesterday. She said it would be a bad example for the rest of the patients in this ward. So I have not broken any rules. But if you gimme a cigarette, I sure will smoke it."

"I will not give you a cigarette," I said.

"O.K.," said Simple. "You will want me to do something for you someday."

"You have everything you need right here in this hospital," I said. "You know if you really needed something you are supposed to have, I would bring it."

"They feed me pretty good in here," said Simple. "Only one thing I do not like—they won't let you take your own bath."

"And what is wrong about that?"

"Well, the morning nurse, she comes in before day A.M. and grabs you by the head. When she gets through scrubbing your ears they feel just like they have been shucked. Ain't nobody washed my ears so hard since I got out from under my mother."

"Sleepy-headed as you are, I guess she is just trying to wake you up."

"And, man," said Simple, "when she washes your stomach, it tickles. I told her I was ticklish and not to touch me nowhere near my ribs, nor my navel."

"I do not see why a big husky fellow like you should be ticklish."

"I do not mind when she rubs my back, though. That alcohol sure smells fine."

"Reminds you of something to drink, I presume?"

"It do feel sort of cool and good like the last drop of a gin rickey. But I don't want to think of gin rickey now, pal."

"I shouldn't think you would," I said. "That is why you

are here— becoming intoxicated and forgetting your overcoat."

"That is not true," said Simple. "I got mad. Joyce made
me so mad I walked out of the house at one A.M. without
my coat and the wind was frantic that night. Zero! But
being drunk had nothing to do with it. A woman aggra-
vates a man, drunk or sober. But Joyce is sorry now that
she ever mentioned Zarita. She come here yesterday and
told me so. She is sorry she done caused me to get pneumonia. She knows Zarita ain't nothing to me even if she
did accidentally see me talking to her through the vestibule. But I do not want to discuss how come I am in this
hospital. I *am* here. I *am* sick. And I cannot get out of this
bed. Why do you reckon they make these hospital beds so
high?"

"To keep people from getting out easily," I said.

"Well, they are so high that if a man ever *fell* out, he
would break his neck. I am even afraid to turn over in this
bed. I naturally sleeps restless, but this bed is so high I
am scared to sleep restless, so I lay here stiff as a board and
don't close my eyes. I mean I am really stiff when morning
comes! This would be a right nice bed if it was not so
narrow and so hard and so high."

"Everything must be wrong with that bed," I said, "to
hear you tell it."

"I don't see why they don't make hospital beds more
comfortable. In a place where people have to *stay* in bed,
they ought to have a feather mattress like Aunt Lucy used
to have."

"If hospital beds were that comfortable," I said, "folks
might never want to go home."

"I would, because I don't like even a pretty nurse to be washing my ears. That is one reason I was glad when I growed up, so I could wash my own ears, and comb my own head."

"Has any nurse here tried to comb your hair?" I inquired.

"These nurses are not crazy," said Simple. "My head is tender! Man, nobody here better not try to pull a comb through my hair but me. If they do, I will get up out of this bed—no matter how high it is—and carry my bohunkus on home."

"Calm down," I said. "You'll run your temperature up. Nobody is going to comb your hair, man."

"You can certainly think of some unpleasant subjects," said Simple. "Even if I was dying, I would comb my own head—and better not nobody else touch it! But say, boy, if you want to do me a favor, when you come back bring me a stocking-cap to make my hair lay down. That is one thing these white folks do not have in this hospital. I wonder if it is against the rules to wear a nylon stocking-cap in this here high bed? If it ain't, you tell Joyce to send me one."

"Very well."

"Also a small drink, because you know it's a long time between drinks in a hospital. And sometimes I don't have nothing to do but lay here and think. The other day I got to thinking about the Age of the Air when rocket planes get to be common."

"What did you think about it?"

"About how women will have a hard time keeping up with their husbands then," said Simple.

"How's that?"

"Mens will have girl friends all over the world, not just around the corner where a wife can find out—and sue for divorce. Why, when rocket planes get to be as cheap as Fords, I'm liable to go calling in Cairo any week end."

"Joyce would be right behind you," I said.

"I expect so. Not even in a rocket plane could I keep Joyce from knowing my whereabouts. But you know what I am talking about is true, and in the future it is going to be even better. In 1975, when a man can get in a rocket plane and shoot through the stratosphere a thousand miles a minute—when he can get to London sooner than I can get from Harlem to Times Square—you know, and I know, a guy will meet some woman he likes halfway across the earth in Australia and any night after dinner he will shoot over there to see her while he tells his wife he's going out to play pool. He can be back by bedtime."

"Your imagination is certainly far-fetched," I said.

"No place will be far-fetched when them rocket planes gets perfected," said Simple. "If I can afford it, I sure will own one myself. Then, in my rocket I will rock! You won't see me hanging around no Harlem bars no more. Saturday nights I will rock on down to Rio and drink coconut milk and gin with them Brazilian chicks whilst dancing a samba. Sunday morning I will zoom on over to Africa and knock out some palm wine before I come back to Seventh Avenue around noon to eat some of Joyce's chicken and dumplings.

"Joyce will say, 'Jess, where you been this morning with your hair blowed back so slick?'

"I will say, 'Nowheres, baby, but just out for a little ride in the clouds to clean the cobwebs out of my brain. I drunk a little too much in Hong Kong last night. And don't you know, after them Chinese bars closed the sky was so crowded, it took me nearly ten minutes to fly back to Harlem to get an aspirin. So this morning, baby, I didn't fly nowheres but straight up in them nice cool clouds for a breath of fresh air, then right back home to you.' "

"What are you going to say if Joyce smells that African palm wine on your breath?" I asked.

"How do you know anybody can smell palm wine?" said Simple. "Maybe by that time somebody will have invented something to take the scent out of *all* lickers anyhow. Besides, I won't be drinking enough to get drunk. I'd be very careful with my rocket plane so as not to run into some planet, neither no star. I will keep a clear head in the air."

"That is more than you keep on earth, except when you're in the hospital."

"There you go low-rating me," sighed Simple. "But listen, daddy-o, such another scrambling of races as there is going to be when they gets that rocket plane perfected! Why, when a man can shoot from Athens, Georgia, to Athens, Greece, in less than an hour, you know there is going to be intermarriage. I am liable to marry a Greek myself."

"Are there any colored Greeks?"

"I would not be prejudiced toward color," said Simple, rising on his pillow, "and if I did not like the licker they drink in Greece, I would fly to Nagasaki and drink saki. Or I might come back to Harlem and have a beer with you."

"If you're doing all that flying around, what makes you think I would remain here in Harlem? I might be out in my rocket, too."

"Great stuff, daddy-o! We might bump into each other over London—who knows? Because I sure would be rocking through the sky. Why, man, I would rock so far away from this color line in the U.S.A., till it wouldn't be funny. I might even build me a garage on Mars and a mansion on Venus. On summer nights I would scoot down the Milky Way just to cool myself off. I would not have no old-time jet-propelled plane either. My plane would run on atom power. This earth I would not bother with no more. No, buddy-o! The sky would be my roadway and the stars my stopping place. Man, if I had a rocket plane, I would rock off into space and be solid gone. Gone. Real gone! I mean *gone!*"

"I think you are gone now," I said. "Out of your head."

"Not quite," said Simple.

21

Final Fear

The next time I visited Simple, I found him convalescent, slightly ashy and a bit thinner, sitting up in bed, but low in spirits. He was gazing sadly at the inscription on a comic book, *"Lovingly yours, Joyce."*

"She has just been here," he said, "and I feel like I am going to have a relapse."

"If that's the way visitors affect you, then I will depart."

"Not all visitors," said Simple, "just Joyce. I love that girl."

"Then why does a visit from her get you down?"

"A woman brought me into this world," said Simple, "and I do believe women will take me out. They is the fault of my being in this hospital with pneumonia because my doctor told me the mind is worse than my body and from the looks of my chest, I must of been worrying."

"So you too have one of those fashionable psychosomatic illnesses," I said.

"No, it's Zarita and Isabel," said Simple, "plus Joyce. That wife of mine called me up New Year's Eve just when I was starting out to have some fun—long-distance, *collect*, from Baltimore—just to tell me that since another year was starting, she was tired of being tied to me and not being *with* me. She told me again either to come back to her or else get her a divorce. I said which would she rather have after all these years, me or the divorce.

"She said, 'Divorce!'

"I said, 'How much do a divorce cost nowadays?'

"She said, 'Three Hundred Dollars.'

"That is what I am feeling bad about, buddy-o. If I had not paid Five Dollars to marry that woman in the past, I would not have to pay Three Hundred now to get loose."

"Maybe it would be cheaper to go back to her."

"My nerves is wrecked," said Simple. "That woman is incontemptible. She has caused me mental anguish, also a headache. I will not go back. Besides, Joyce has been too good to me for me to cut out now. You see them flowers she brought to this hospital, also these two comic books and four packs of chewing gum. But Joyce is also a headache."

"You are just weak from your recent illness," I said.

"You mean Joyce is weak for me," corrected Simple. "Sitting right here on this bed today, she told me she is not built of bricks. Joyce says she's got a heart, also a soul, and is respectable. Joyce swears she is getting tired of me coming to her house so regular and everybody asking when is we gonna marry. She says I've been setting in her parlor too late for her respectability.

"I said, 'One o'clock ain't late.'

"She said, 'No, but two and three o'clock is, and you sure can't stay till four.'

"I said, 'Baby, it ain't what you do, it's how you do it.' But she disagreed.

"She said, 'No, it ain't what you do—it's what folks *think* you do. When folks see you coming out of my place at two-three-four o'clock in the morning, you know what they think—even if it ain't so. I have been knowing you too long not to be married to you. It were not just day before yesterday that we met,' Joyce says."

"Then a divorce would be good for both of you," I interjected. "You could get all those day-before-yesterdays straightened out."

"Days is like stair-steps," said Simple. "If you stumbled on the first day yesterday, you liable to be still falling tomorrow. I have stumbled."

"Anyhow," I said, "it is better to fall up than to fall down. You can get things straightened out when you get well."

"No matter what a man does, sick or well, something is always liable to happen," said Simple, "especially if you are colored."

"Race has nothing to do with it," I said. "In this uncertain world, something unpleasant can happen to anybody, colored or white, regardless of race."

"Um-hum," said Simple. "You can be robbed and mugged in the night—even choked."

"That's right," I said, "or you can get poisoned from drinking King Kong after hours."

"Sure can," said Simple. "Or you *can* go crazy from worriation."

"Or lose your job."

"Else your money on the horses."

"Or on numbers."

"Or policy."

"Or on Chinese lottery, if you live on the Coast."

"Or poker or blackjack or pokino or tonk. And you ain't mentioned Georgia skin," said Simple.

"I can't play skin," I said.

"It's a rugged card game," said Simple. "If I had never learnt it, I might be rich today. But skin's a mere skimption compared to some of the things that can happen to a man. For instant, if you was a porter, your train could wreck. If you was in the Merchant Marines, your boat could sink. Or if you're a aviator, you're liable to run into the Empire State Building or Abyssinia Baptist Church and bust up your plane. It is awful, man, what can happen to you in this life!"

"You talk as though you've had a hard time," I said. "Have any of those things ever happened to you?"

"What're you talking about?" cried Simple, sitting bolt upright in bed. "Not only am I half dead right now from pneumonia, but everything else *has* happened to me! I have been cut, shot, stabbed, run over, hit by a car, and tromped by a horse. I have also been robbed, fooled, deceived, two-timed, double-crossed, dealt seconds, and mighty near blackmailed—but I am still here!"

"You're a tough man," I said.

"I have been fired, laid off, and last week given an indefinite vacation, also Jim Crowed, segregated, barred out, insulted, eliminated, called black, yellow, and red, locked in, locked out, locked up, also left holding the bag. I have been caught in the rain, caught in raids, caught short with my rent, and caught with another man's wife. In my time I have been caught—but I am still here!"

"You have suffered," I said.

"Suffered!" cried Simple. "My mama should have named me Job instead of Jess Semple. I have been under-fed, underpaid, undernourished, and everything but *undertaken*. I been bit by dogs, cats, mice, rats, poll parrots, fleas, chiggers, bedbugs, granddaddies, mosquitoes, and a gold-toothed woman."

"Great day in the morning!"

"That ain't all," said Simple. "In this life I been abused, confused, misused, accused, false-arrested, tried, sentenced, paroled, blackjacked, beat, third-degreed, and near about lynched!"

"Anyhow, your health has been good—up to now," I said.

"Good health nothing," objected Simple, waving his hands, kicking off the cover, and swinging his feet out of bed. "I done had everything from flat feet to a flat head. Why, man, I was born with the measles! Since then I had smallpox, chickenpox, whooping cough, croup, appendicitis, athlete's foot, tonsillitis, arthritis, backache, mumps, and a strain—but I am still here. Daddy-o, I'm still here!"

"Having survived all that, what are you afraid of, now that you are almost over pneumonia?"

"I'm afraid," said Simple, "I will die before my time."

22

There Ought to Be a Law

"I have been up North a long time, but it looks like I just cannot learn to like white folks."

"I don't care to hear you say that," I said, "because there are a lot of good white people in this world."

"Not enough of them," said Simple, waving his evening paper. "If there was, they would make this American country good. But just look at what this paper is full of."

"You cannot dislike *all* white people for what the bad ones do," I said. "And I'm certain you don't dislike them all because once you told me yourself that you wouldn't wish any harm to befall Mrs. Roosevelt."

"Mrs. Roosevelt is different," said Simple.

"There now! You see, you are talking just as some white people talk about the Negroes they *happen* to like. They are always 'different.' That is a provincial way to think. You need to get around more."

"You mean among white folks?" asked Simple. "How can I make friends with white folks when they got Jim Crow all over the place?"

"Then you need to open your mind."

"I have near about *lost* my mind worrying with them," said Simple. "In fact, they have hurt my soul."

"You certainly feel bad tonight," I said. "Maybe you need a drink."

"Nothing in a bottle will help my soul," said Simple, "but I will take a drink."

"Maybe it will help your mind," I said. "Beer?"

"Yes."

"Glass or bottle?"

"A bottle because it contains two glasses," said Simple, spreading his paper out on the bar. "Look here at these headlines, man, where Congress is busy passing laws. While they're making all these laws, it looks like to me they ought to make one setting up a few Game Preserves for Negroes."

"What ever gave you that fantastic idea?" I asked.

"A movie short I saw the other night," said Simple, "about how the government is protecting wild life, preserving fish and game, and setting aside big tracts of land where nobody can fish, shoot, hunt, nor harm a single living creature with furs, fins, or feathers. But it did not show a thing about Negroes."

"I thought you said the picture was about 'wild life.' Negroes are not wild."

"No," said Simple, "but we need protection. This film showed how they put aside a thousand acres out West where the buffaloes roam and nobody can shoot a single one of them. If they do, they get in jail. It also showed some big National Park with government airplanes dropping food down to the deers when they got snowed under and had nothing to eat. The government protects and takes care of buffaloes and deers—which is more than the government does for me or my kinfolks down South. Last

month they lynched a man in Georgia and just today I
see where the Klan has whipped a Negro within a inch
of his life in Alabama. And right up North here in New
York a actor is suing a apartment house that won't even
let a Negro go up on the elevator to see his producer. That
is what I mean by Game Preserves for Negroes—Congress ought to set aside some place where we can go and
nobody can jump on us and beat us, neither lynch us nor
Jim Crow us every day. Colored folks rate as much protection as a buffalo, or a deer."

"You have a point there," I said.

"This here movie showed great big beautiful lakes with
signs up all around:

NO FISHING — STATE GAME PRESERVE

But it did not show a single place with a sign up:

NO LYNCHING

It also showed flocks of wild ducks settling down in a nice
green meadow behind a government sign that said:

NO HUNTING

It were nice and peaceful for them fish and ducks. There
ought to be some place where it is nice and peaceful for
me, too, even if I am not a fish or a duck.

"They showed one scene with two great big old long-
horn elks locking horns on a Game Preserve somewhere
out in Wyoming, fighting like mad. Nobody bothered them
elks or tried to stop them from fighting. But just let me get
in a little old fist fight here in this bar, they will lock me
up and the Desk Sergeant will say, 'What are you colored
boys doing, disturbing the peace?' Then they will give me

thirty days and fine me twice as much as they would a white man for doing the same thing. There ought to be some place where I can fight in peace and not get fined them high fines."

"You disgust me," I said. "I thought you were talking about a place where you could be quiet and compose your mind. Instead, you are talking about fighting."

"I would like a place where I could do both," said Simple. "If the government can set aside some spot for a elk *to be a elk* without being bothered, or a fish *to be a fish* without getting hooked, or a buffalo *to be a buffalo* without being shot down, there ought to be some place in this American country where a Negro can be a Negro without being Jim Crowed. There ought to be a law. The next time I see my congressman, I am going to tell him to introduce a bill for Game Preserves for Negroes."

"The Southerners would filibuster it to death," I said.

"If we are such a problem to them Southerners," said Simple, "I should think they would want some place to preserve us out of their sight. But then, of course, you have to take into consideration that if the Negroes was taken out of the South, who would they lynch? What would they do for sport? A Game Preserve is for to keep people from bothering anything that is living.

"When that movie finished, it were sunset in Virginia and it showed a little deer and its mama laying down to sleep. Didn't nobody say, 'Get up, deer, you can't sleep here,' like they would to me if I was to go to the White Sulphur Springs Hotel."

" 'The foxes have holes, and the birds of the air have

nests; but the Son of man hath not where to lay his head.' "

"That is why I want a Game Preserve for Negroes," said Simple.

23

Income Tax

On March 14th, just the day before his taxes came due, Simple was sitting in a booth across from the bar, figuring, and each time he figured he put his pencil in his mouth.

"Joyce's Fifty-Nine-Dollar birthday wrist watch on time, plus Two Dollars and Seventy-Five Cents cab fare to the Bronx for that wedding reception to which we was late, minus Twenty-Nine Dollars and Eleven Cents old-age dependency insurance, plus miscellaneous Five Hundred and Seventy-Nine Dollars and Twenty-Two Cents, minus One Dollar and Fifteen Cents work-clothes deduction—man! I ain't *never* gonna get it straight."

"What's all this high finance," I said, "concerning birthday watches and nondeductible cab fare?"

"Income tax," said Simple. "I deducts all."

"Pshaw! Just think of the movie stars and Wall Street people who really have to worry about income tax," I said.

"I don't care nothing about them folks," answered Simple. "All I know is that tomorrow the man is *demanding* —not asking—for money that I not only don't have—but ain't even seen."

"The Bureau of Internal Revenue seldom makes mistakes, Jess. If it does, they've got people to check and recheck, and if they miscalculate even as little as two cents, you'll eventually get it back."

"I just like to check for myself," said Simple. "So I been figuring on this thing for three days and it still don't come out right. Instead of them owing me, looks like I owe them something which I don't know where I'm going to get."

"Why didn't you just take your figures to a public accountant and let him figure it out for you?"

"Man, I took 'em to one of them noteriety republicans once and he charged me so much I got discouraged."

"Maybe next year things will be different, old man. According to the papers, Congress is considering a bill to reduce taxes."

"By the time Congress convenes, I'll be without means," said Simple. "Besides, I don't get enough for my taxes. I wants to vote down South. It's hell to pay taxes when I can't even vote down home."

" 'Taxation without representation is tyranny,' so the books say."

"Sure is!" said Simple. "I don't see why Negroes down South should pay taxes a-tall. You know Buddy Jones' brother, what was wounded in the 92nd in Italy, don't you? Well, he was telling me about how bad them rednecks treated him when he was in the army in Mississippi. He said he don't never want to see no parts of the South again. He were born and raised in Yonkers and not used to such stuff. Now his nerves is shattered. He can't even stand a Southern accent no more."

"Jim Crow shock," I said. "I guess it can be as bad as shell shock."

"It can be worse," said Simple. "Jim Crow happens to men every day down South, whereas a man's not in a battle every day. Buddy's brother has been out of the army three years and he's still sore about Mississippi."

"What happened to him down there?"

"I will tell it to you like it was told to me," said Simple. "You know Buddy's brother is a taxicab driver, don't you? Well, the other day he was telling me he was driving his cab downtown on Broadway last week when a white man hailed him, got in, and then said in one of them slow Dixie drawls, "Bouy, tek me ovah to Fefty-ninth Street and Fefth Avahnue.'

"Buddy's brother told him, 'I ain't gonna take you no-where. Get outta my cab—and quick!'

"The white man didn't know what was the matter so he says, 'Why?'

"Buddy's brother said, 'Because I don't like Southerners, that's why! You treated me so mean when I was in the army down South that I don't never want to see none of you-all no more. And I *sure* don't like to hear you talk. It goes all through me. I spent eighteen months in hell in Mississippi.'

"The white man got red in the face, also mad, and called a cop to make Buddy's brother drive him where he wanted to go. The cop was one of New York's finest, a great big Irishman. The copper listened to the man, then he listened to Buddy's brother. Setting right there in his taxi at 48th and Broadway, Buddy's brother told that cop all about Mississippi, how he was Jim Crowed on the train on the way down going to drill for Uncle Sam, how he was Jim Crowed in camp, also how whenever he had a furlough, him and his colored buddies had to wait and *wait* and WAIT at the camp gate for a bus to get to town because they filled the busses up with white soldiers and the colored soldiers just had to stand behind and wait. Sometimes on payday if there were a big crowd of white soldiers, the colored G.I.'s would never get to town at all.

" 'Officer, I'm telling you,' Buddy's brother said, 'that Mississippi is something! Down South they don't have no nice polices like you. Down South all them white cops want to do is beat a Negro's head, cuss you, and call you names. They do not protect Americans if they are black. They lynched a man five miles down the road from our camp one night and left him hanging there for three days as a warning, so they said, to us Northern Negroes to know how to act in the South, particularly if from New York.'

"Meanwhile the Southern white man who was trying to get the cop to make Buddy's brother drive him over to Fifth Avenue was getting redder and redder. He said, 'You New York Negras need to learn how to act.'

" 'Shut up!' says the cop. 'This man is talking.'

"Buddy's brother talked on. 'Officer,' he says, 'it were so bad in that army camp that I will tell you a story of something that happened to me. They had us colored troops quartered way down at one end of the camp, six miles back from the gate, up against the levee. One day they sent me to do some yard work up in the white part of the camp. My bladder was always weak, so I had to go to the latrine no sooner than I got there. Everything is separated in Mississippi, even latrines, with signs up WHITE and COLORED. But there wasn't any COLORED latrine anywhere around, so I started to go in one marked WHITE.

" 'A cracker M.P. yelled at me, *'Halt!'*

" 'When I didn't halt—because I couldn't—he drew his gun on me and cocked it. He threatened to shoot me if I went in that WHITE latrine.

" 'Well, he made me so mad, I walked all the way back to my barracks and got a gun myself. I came back and I walked up to that Southern M.P. I said, *'Neither you nor me will never see no Germans nor no Japs if you try to stop me from going in this latrine this morning.'*

" 'That white M.P. didn't try to stop me. He just turned pale, and I went in. But by that time, officer, I was so mad I decided to set down and stay awhile. So I did. With my gun on my lap, I just sat—and every time a Southerner came in, I cocked the trigger. Ain't nobody said a word. They just looked at me and walked out. I stayed there as long as I wanted to—black as I am—in that WHITE latrine. Down in Mississippi a colored soldier has to have a gun even to go to the toilet! So, officer, that is why I do not want to ride this man—because he is one of them that wouldn't even let me go in their latrines down South, do you understand?'

" 'Understand?' says the cop, 'Of course, I understand. Be jeezus! It's like that exactly that the damned English did the Irish. Faith, you do not have to haul him. . . . Stranger, get yerself another cab. Scram, now! Quick—before I run you in.'

"That white man hauled tail! And Buddy's brother drove off saluting that cop—and blowing his horn for New York City. But me, if I'd of been there," said Simple, "I would of asked that officer just one thing about Ireland. I would have said, 'Well, before you-all got free—kicked around as you was—did you still have to pay taxes to the British?' "

"I can answer that for you," I said. "Of course, the Irish had to pay taxes. All colonial peoples have to pay taxes to their rulers."

"How do you know?" asked Simple. "You ain't Irish."

"No," I said, "but I read books."

"You don't learn everything in books," said Simple.

"It wouldn't hurt you to read one once in a while," I said.

"Not to change the subject, but I need a beer to help me figure up this income tax," said Simple. "Bartender, a couple of beers on my friend here—who reads books."

"I do not like your tone of voice," I said. "I will not pay for beer to entertain a man who has nothing but contempt for the written word."

"Buddy-o, daddy-o, pal, I do not want to argue with you this evening because I haven't got time. You are colored just like me, so set down and help me figure up my taxes for these white folks. What did you say that book says about taxation?"

"Without representation, it's tyranny."

"If you don't know how to add, subtract, multiply, erase, deduct, steal, stash, save, conceal, and long-divide, it is worse than that," said Simple. "Taxes is *hell!* Buddy-o, here's our beer."

"It seems to me you should understand mathematics," I said. "You've been to school."

"I didn't learn much," said Simple, "which is why I have to run my feet off all day long and work hard. What your head don't *under*stand, your feet have to stand."

"Well, you certainly have opinions about everything under the sun," I said. "You ought to have a newspaper since you have so much to say."

"I can talk," said Simple, "but I can't write."

"Then you ought to be an orator."

"Uh-um, I'm scared of the public. My place is at the bar."

"Of Justice?"

"Justice don't run no bar."

24

No Alternative

"Man, you don't know how I have suffered these last few weeks," Simple groaned into an empty glass. "Joyce's birthday, the Urban League ball we had to go to, income tax, hospital bill, and so forth—"

"What's 'and so forth'?" I asked.

"My landlady," said Simple. "That woman has no respect for her roomers a-tall. In fact, she cares less for her roomers than she does for her dog."

"What kind of dog has she got?"

"A little old houndish kind of dog," said Simple. "But is she crazy about that hound! She will put a roomer out— dead out in the street—when he does not pay his rent, but she does not put out that dog, not even when it chews up her favorite Teddy bear which her second husband give her for her birthday. That dog is her heart. She would feed that dog before she would feed me. When I went down in the kitchen last week to give her my room rent, I saw her hand Trixie a whole chicken leg—and she did not offer me a bite."

"Were you hungry?" I asked.

"I could have used a drumstick," said Simple. "It would

have meant more to me than it did to that little fice."

"I gather you do not like dogs."

"I love dogs," said Simple. "When my landlady was laid up with arthritis and scared to get her feet wet, I even took that little old she-hound of hers out two or three times to the park to do its duty—although I would not be seen with no dog like that if it belonged to me. All I got was, 'Thank you, you certainly nice, Mr. Semple.' She used my real last name, all formal and everything. 'You certainly nice, yes, indeed.' But did I get a extra towel when I asked for it? I did not. All I got was, 'Laundries is high and towels is scarce.' Yet I seen her dry that dog on a nice big white bath towel, the likes of which she never give a roomer yet. I don't think that is right, to care less about roomers than you do about a dog, do you?"

"Ties between a dog and its master are often greater than human ties."

"Ties, nothing," said Simple. "That lazy little old mutt don't bring her in a thing, not even a bone. I bring in Ten Dollars rent each and every week—even if it is a little late."

"You got behind though, didn't you, when you weren't working?"

"I *tried* to get behind," said Simple, "but she did not let me get far. I told her they was changing from a ball-bearing plant to a screw factory and it might even take three months. But she said it better not take *three weeks*—do, and she would get eviction orders and evict me. So I had to go to the post office and draw out my little money and lay it on the line. That very evening she says, 'Oh, this poor dog ain't been out of the house in five days, bad as my knees ache.' So me, like a chump, I take it out to the park."

"Why doesn't her husband take care of it?" I asked.

"He runs on the road," said Simple. "When he gets through taking care of white folks, he does not feel like taking care of dogs. Harlem is no place for dogs—people do not have time to look after them."

"True," I said, "but Harlemites love dogs, and there are a great many here."

"Almost as many as there are roomers," agreed Simple. "But it is not good for the dogs, because people work all day and leave the dog by itself. A dog gets lonesome just like a human. He wants to associate with other dogs, but when they take him out, the poor dog is on a leash and cannot run around. They won't even let him rub noses with another dog, or pick out his own tree. Now, that is not good for a dog. For instant, take Trixie, my landlady's hound. Spring is coming. I asked her one day last week had Trixie ever been married.

"My landlady says, 'You mean mated?'

"I says, 'Yes, I was just trying to be polite.'

"She says, 'No, indeed! Trixie is a virgin.'

"Now, ain't that awful! That poor dog never had a chance in life, which worried me. So I said, 'Next time I take Trixie to the park, I will see that she meets some gentleman dogs.'

"But, man, don't you know that woman hollered like she had been shot. She says, 'No, indeed, you won't! I do not want Trixie all crossed up with no low-breeded curs.'

"I says, 'You must be prejudiced, madam. Is Trixie got a pedigree?'

"My landlady says, 'She is pure Spotted Dutch Brindle.'

"Before I thought, I said, 'Pure mutt.'

"My landlady jumped salty, I mean salty! She reined in Trixie and yelled, 'You will apologize to this dog, Mr. Semple, else leave my house.' "

"Did you apologize to that dog?"

"I had no alternity. Hard as rooms is to find these days, I do not know which is worse, to be a roomer or a dog."

25

Question Period

"I know one thing," said Simple, "I am sick and tired of radio commentators who don't talk sense."

"Now what's the matter?"

"Aw, Joyce took me to one of them Town Hall lectures the other night and I ain't been the same since. I wouldn't a been caught dead ten blocks near nothing like that if it hadn't been for Joyce. Trust a woman like she is to drag me out in the cold to hear a commentator *in person* when I could've stayed home and heard one on the radio—if I'd a wanted to hear one—just as well."

"A commentator?" I asked.

"A commentator," said Simple. "He's been all over the world and saw the war, atomic bombs exploding, also the conversation of the Nazis to democracy, and stuff like that. He had a whole lot of facts and figures to prove it, too. His subject was 'The World Situation.' "

"Was he penetrating?"

"Joyce made me pay a Dollar Six Bits a head to penetrate other folks' troubles."

"What's wrong with that?" I asked. "I think it was a good idea for Joyce to take you. You need an awareness of world affairs."

"I'm aware, all right," said Simple. "Aware that it costs half of my weekly beer money to hear about problems in foreign countries when I got a Million Dollars' worth of my own! I'm aware that folks are mistreated and starvin' right here at home. They whip my head and poke my eyes out with a billy-club down South. The Ku Klux Klan is trying to scare colored folks out of voting—but I don't hear them lecture commentators talking about that!"

"They overlook a number of pertinent topics," I said, "which simply indicates that the equilibrium of current sociological equations is somewhat irregular."

"Somewhat?" yelled Simple. "Man, for a Dollar Seventy-Five Cents a ticket, that commentator should at least have mentioned lynching that Negro the other day and nobody doing nothing about it."

"I suppose they had a question period after the lecture?"

"They sure did," said Simple. "Joyce wanted to ask a question, but she was ashamed to get up and ask it herself. She kept nudging me in the ribs and telling me to read it off for her since she had it all written down beforehand. I told her if she wanted to know so bad, why didn't she get up and read it herself. But she said she was shy. I said, 'Ain't this a killer. You won't ask him nothing—but it's O.K. for *me* to get up and make a fool out of myself.' "

"Well, did you get up and ask her question?"

"I did not," said Simple. "I figured if I was going to be stared at, I might as well use my *own* brains and ask a question for myself."

"What was your question?"

"I raised my hand and said, 'Mr. Commentator, how come you fellows always know so much about them foreign countries which you can analyze so easy, but when somebody asks you what's going on here as I have before now thought about mailing several questions in to you on the radio and got no answer, don't you have no realization of how bad my colored condition is?' "

"What did he say?"

"He hemmed and hawed and said what was happening in other countries stirred the consciousness of the world more than what went on here at home and that Negroes had to take a long view. So I told him a whipped head was a *whipped* head—no matter whose shoulders it was on, in Europe or here. And if it was on *my* shoulders, that made it twice as bad—I didn't care how long the view was. I also told him that if Negroes' being mistreated *right under his nose* didn't stir his consciousness, then he must be unconscious."

"What happened then?" I asked.

"That near about broke up the forum," said Simple. "Joyce started pulling on my sleeve and talking about 'Now! Now! Set down. You're not the speaker!' "

"If your question caused so much disturbance," I said, "I am curious to know what question Joyce wanted to ask. Is her slip of paper still in your pocket?"

"Yes, right here," said Simple. "Look. With pork chops as high as they are in Harlem, Joyce was going to ask the man, 'If the United Nations took over Trieste, would they also internationalize the suburbs or would the outskirts of town still belong to Yugoslavia, and if so, how far?' That is what Joyce was going to ask!"

26

Lingerie

"Where are you going?" I asked as I bumped into Simple on 125th Street near the Baby Grand.

"I have been where I am going," said Simple.

"At Joyce's?"

"Natch. But she were in a very impatient mood tonight," said Simple as we walked up Eighth Avenue. "Her and another girl were there sewing like mad, so Joyce did not care much about having a gentleman caller. She were busy."

"Joyce sees you practically every night, so no wonder," I said. "You are hardly in the category of a caller. What were they making?"

"Lin-ger-ies," said Simple. "Some friend girl of Joyce's is getting married Sunday, so they are making her some step-ins and step-outs, also some slips, for a present. The other girl were making what she called a bood-war gown —but it looked like a nightgown to me. Joyce says there is nothing so fine as a real handmade lin-ger-ies. And everything were pink. I asked them how come ladies' lin-ger-ies is always pink.

"Joyce said, 'What do you mean, *always?*'

"I said, 'Just about all I ever saw is pink.'

"Joyce says, 'You has no business seeing so much. Besides, that is no fit subject for a man, especially in front of company.'

"She never did answer my question. Maybe you can tell me, daddy-o, why is women's underneath-wears practically *always* pink? For instant, why ain't teddies sometimes light green?"

"I have seen them black," I said.

"I don't mean when they need washing," said Simple. "Nine times out of ten, a girl's lin-ger-ies is pink. I want to know why."

"Let me think a minute and come to some logical conclusion," I stalled. "There must be a reason. I never thought of it before."

"I have never seen purple ones," said Simple. "They is pink—always pink!"

"Maybe the word *lingerie* means *pink* in French," I said.

"Then it must mean *pink* in English, too," said Simple, "because every time a dame says lin-ger-ies, it's something pink—from brassieres to girdles to garters to pants."

"I think I have the reason," I said. "Listen, lingerie was probably invented by Caucasians, so they dyed it pink to blend with the rosy tint of a white woman's complexion."

"That could be so," said Simple. "It sure could! White folks make everything else to suit themselves. But since Negroes ain't pink, why don't Joyce make her friend girl some chocolate-colored sepia-tan lin-ger-ies, because that girl is a nice chocolate-brown. Also *real gone!* I mean a pretty Ethiopian Abyssinimon brown!"

"Are you acquainted with her?"

"I have met her," said Simple, "and in my mind's eyes, I can see that chick right now slipping her chocolate hips into a pair of chocolate step-ins, then sliding her sepia shoulders into a chocolate slip."

"You have a vivid imagination," I said.

"Vivian's not her name. It's *Jean*. And when she gets ready to retire, to dream, relax, lay down, Jean could ease her fine brown frame into a chocolate gown. Man, chocolate is better than pink, any day."

"You are a race man for true," I said. "For you, even lingerie should be *colored,* with a capital *C*."

"It should be," said Simple. "I am going to tell Joyce to make that girl some tan-skin things for her present."

"You're fixing to anger Joyce," I said, "taking an intimate interest in some girl you hardly know."

"She *is* kinder jealous-hearted," said Simple. "But next time I go back to pay Joyce a call—which will be around dinner time tomorrow, since I don't board with Joyce, just accepts her hospitality—I am going to tell her that I have found out why lin-ger-ies is pink."

"Thanks to me," I said.

"Yes, thanks to you," said Simple. "Now I will thank you for a beer. I lent Joyce my last Two Dollars to buy some lace on that girl's gown—which were a mistake because now that spring is coming and she's helping her friend girl to get her honeymoon clothes together, Joyce has done started thinking about a June wedding herself."

"Does Joyce want you to commit bigamy?"

"She knows I can't commit nothing without a divorce," said Simple.

27

Spring Time

"I wish that spring would come more often now that it is
here," said Simple.

"How could it come more often?"

"It could if God had made it that-a-way," said Simple.
"I also wish it would last longer."

"It looks as if you would prefer spring all the year
around."

"Just most of the year," said Simple. "As it is now,
summer comes too soon and winter lasts too long. I do not
like real hot weather, neither cold. I like spring."

"Spring is too changeable for me—sometimes hot, sometimes cold."

"I am not talking about that kind of spring," said
Simple. "I mean June-time spring when it is just nice and
mellow—like a cool drink."

"Of what?"

"Anything," said Simple. "Anything that is strong as
the sun and cool as the moon. But I am not talking about
drinking now. I am talking about spring. Oh, it is wonderful! It is the time when flowers come out of their buds,
birds come out of their nests, bees come out of their hives,

Negroes come out of their furnished rooms, and butter-
flies out of their cocoons."

"Also snakes come out of their holes."

"They is little young snakes," said Simple, "else big old
sleepy snakes that ain't woke up good yet till the sun strikes
them. That is why I do not like summer, because the sun
is so hot it makes even a cold snake mad. Spring is my
season. Summer was made to give you a taste of what hell
is like. Fall was made for the clothing-store people to
coin money because every human has to buy a overcoat,
muffler, heavy socks, and gloves. Winter was made for
landladies to charge high rents and keep cold radiators and
make a fortune off of poor tenants. But spring! Throw your
overcoat on the pawnshop counter, tell the landlady to kiss
your foot, open your windows, let the fresh air in. Me, myself, I love spring!

"Why, if I was down home now, daddy-o, I would get
out my fishing pole and take me a good old Virginia ham
sandwich and go set on the banks of the river all day and
just dream and fish and fish and dream. I might have me
a big old quart bottle of beer tied on a string down in the
water to keep cool, and I would just fish and dream and
dream and fish."

"You would not have any job?" I asked.

"I would respect work just like I respected my mother
and not hit her a lick. I would be far away from all this
six A.M. alarm-clock business, crowded subways, gulping
down my coffee to get to the man's job in time, and working all day shut up inside where you can't even smell the
spring—and me still smelling ether and worried about my
winter hospital bill. If I was down home, buddy-o, I would

pull off my shoes and let my toes air and just set on the riverbank and dream and fish and fish and dream, and I would not worry about no job."

"Why didn't you stay down home when you were there?"

"You know why I didn't stay," said Simple. "I did not like them white folks and they did not like me. Maybe if it wasn't for white folks, I would've stayed down South where spring comes earlier than it do up here. White folks is the cause of a lot of inconveniences in my life."

"They've even driven you away from an early spring."

"It do not come as early in Harlem as it does down South," said Simple, "but it comes. And there ain't no white folks living can keep spring from coming. It comes to Harlem the same as it does downtown, too. Nobody can keep spring out of Harlem. I stuck my head out the window this morning and spring kissed me bang in the face. Sunshine patted me all over the head. Some little old birds was flying and playing on the garbage cans down in the alley, and one of them flew up to the Third Floor Rear and looked at me and cheeped, 'Good morning!'

"I said, 'Bird, howdy-do!'

"Just then I heard my next-door roomer come out of the bathroom so I had to pull my head in from that window and rush to get to the toilet to wash my face before somebody else got there because I did not want to be late to work this morning since today is payday. New York is just rush, rush, rush! But, oh, brother, if I were down home."

"I know—you would just fish and dream and dream and fish."

"And dream and fish and fish and dream!" said Simple. "If spring was to last forever, as sure as my name is Jess, I would just fish and dream."

PART THREE

Hard Times

28

Last Whipping

When I went by his house one Sunday morning to pick up my Kodak that he had borrowed, Simple was standing in the middle of the floor in his shirttail imitating a minister winding up his Sunday morning sermon, gestures and all.

He intoned, " 'Well, I looked and I saw a great beast! And that great beast had its jaws open ready to clamp down on my mortal soul. But I knowed if it was to clamp, ah, my soul would escape and go to glory. Amen! So I was not afraid. My body was afraid, a-a-ah, but my soul was not afraid. My soul said whatsoever you may do to my behind, a-a-ah, beast, you *cannot* harm my soul. Amen! No, Christians! That beast *cannot* tear your immortal soul. That devil in the form of a crocodile, the form of a alligator with a leather hide that slippeth and slideth through the bayous swamp—that alligator *cannot* tear your soul!' "

"You really give a good imitation of a preacher," I said. "But come on and get dressed and let's go, since you say you left my Kodak at Joyce's. I didn't stop by here to hear you preach."

"I am saying that to say this," said Simple, "because

that is the place in the sermon where my old Aunt Lucy jumped up shouting and leapt clean across the pulpit rail and started to preaching herself, right along with the minister.

"She hollered, 'No-ooo-oo-o! Hallelujah, no! It cannot tear your soul. Sometimes the devil comes in human form,' yelled Aunt Lucy, 'sometimes it be's born right into your own family. Sometimes the devil be's your own flesh and kin—and he try your soul—but your soul he cannot tear! Sometimes you be's forced to tear his hide *before* he tears your soul. Amen!'

"Now, Aunt Lucy were talking about *me* that morning when she said 'devil.' That is what I started to tell you."

"Talking about you, why?" I asked.

"Because I had been up to some devilment, and she had done said she was gonna whip me come Monday. Aunt Lucy were so Christian she did not believe in whipping nobody on a Sunday."

"What had you done?"

"Oh, I had just taken one of her best laying hens and give it to a girl who didn't even belong to our church; to roast for her Sunday school picnic, because this old girl said she was aiming to picnic *me*—except that she didn't have nothing good to eat to put in her basket. I was trying to jive this old gal, you know—I was young—so I just took one of Aunt Lucy's hens and give her."

"Why didn't you pick out a pullet that wasn't laying?"

"That hen was the biggest, fattest chicken in the pen —and I wanted that girl to have plenty to pull out of her basket at that picnic so folks would make a great big admiration over her and me."

"How did your Aunt Lucy find out about the hen?"

"Man, you know womenfolks can't keep no secret! That girl told another girl, the other girl told her cousin, the cousin told her mama, her mama told Aunt Lucy—and Aunt Lucy woke me up Sunday morning with a switch in her hand."

"Weren't you too old to be whipped by then?"

"Of course, I was too old to whip—sixteen going on seventeen, big as a ox. But Aunt Lucy did not figure I was grown yet. And she took her duty hard—because she always said the last thing my mother told her when she died was to raise me right."

"What did you do when you saw the switch?"

"Oh, I got all mannish, man. I said, 'Aunt Lucy, you ain't gonna whip me no more. I's a man—and you ain't gonna whip me.'

"Aunt Lucy said, 'Yes, I is, too, Jess. I will whip you until you gets grown enough to know how to act like a man—not just *look* like one. You know you had no business snatching my hen right off her nest and giving it to that low-life hussy what had no better sense than to take it, knowing you ain't got nowhere to get no hen except out of *my* henhouse. Were this not Sunday, I would whale you in a inch of your life before you could get out of that bed.' "

"Aunt Lucy was angry," I commented.

"She was," said Simple. "And big as I was, I was scared. But I was meaning not to let her whip me, even if I had to snatch that sapling out of her hand."

"So what happened on Monday morning?"

"Aunt Lucy waited until I got up, dressed, and washed my face. Then she called me. 'Jess!' I knowed it were whipping time. Just when I was aiming to snatch that switch out of her hand, I seed that Aunt Lucy was crying when she told me to come there. I said, 'Aunt Lucy, what you crying for?'

"She said, 'I am crying 'cause here you is a man, and don't know how to act right yet, and I done did my best to raise you so you would grow up good. I done wore out so many switches on your back, still you tries my soul. But it ain't *my* soul I'm thinking of, son, it's yourn. Jess, I wants you to carry yourself right and 'sociate with peoples what's decent and be a good boy. You understand me? I's getting too old to be using my strength like this. Here!' she hollered, 'bend over and lemme whip you one more time!' "

"Did she whip you?"

"She whipped me—because I bent," said Simple. "When I seen her crying, I would have let her kill me before I raised my hand. When she got through, I said, 'Aunt Lucy, you ain't gonna have to whip me no more. I ain't gonna give you no cause. I do not mind to be beat. But I do not *never* want to see you cry no more—so I am going to do my best to do right from now on and not try your soul. And I am sorry about that hen.'

"And you know, man, from that day to this, I have tried to behave myself. Aunt Lucy is gone to glory this morning, but if she is looking down, she knows that is true. That was my last whipping. But it wasn't the whipping that taught me what I needed to know. It was because she cried—and cried. When peoples care for you and cry for you, they can straighten out your soul. Ain't that right, boy?"

"Yes," I said, "that's right."

29

Nickel for the Phone

"When I were knee-high to a duck I went to the circus and I saw there Jo-Jo the Dog-Faced Boy, or else it were Zip the Pinheaded Man. I never did know the difference because I were too little. I went with my grandpa and grandma before they died and I were sent back to my mama. Neither one of them old folks could read. They also disremembered what the side-show barker said afterwards, so when I got big I never did know if it were Jo-Jo the Dog-Faced Boy I saw or Zip the Pinheaded Man. Anyway, whichever one it were, *he were awful*."

"What makes you think of that now?" I asked.

"Last night Joyce told me I looked like Zip. I am trying to figure out if it *was* Zip that I saw, because if I look like what I saw in that circus, I sure look *bad*."

"You do not have a pinhead," I told him. "But, come to think of it, you could be said to have a dog-face."

"I know I am not good-looking," said Simple, "but I did not think I looked like a dog."

"The last time I saw her, Joyce told me she thought you were a fine-looking man," I said. "Why has she changed her mind?"

"Because I promised to pass by her house night before last night and I did not go."

"Why didn't you?"

"That's my business, but Joyce wants to make it hers. Womens is curious."

"Naturally."

"So when I did not tell her where I went Thursday night, she jumped salty. She said she did not care where I was nohow. So I says, 'Why do you keep on asking me, if you don't care?'

"She says, 'I *did* care, but you have drove all the care out of me, the way you do.' Then she started to cry. Now, when a woman starts to cry, I do not know what to do.

"So I says, 'Let's go down to the corner and have a rum-cola.'

"She says, 'I do not want to go nowhere with you and you looking like Zip!' That is when I started to wondering who Zip were."

"I have always wondered, too," I said, "never having seen that famous freak."

"Another thing I have wondered is, who is Cootie Brown? Last Saturday night somebody said to me, 'Man, you're drunk as Cootie Brown.' "

"Which meant high as a Georgia pine."

"I know what it meant, but I do not know who Cootie Brown was. Do you?"

"I guess he was just somebody who got pretty drunk all the time."

"And Zip were somebody who looked pretty bad all the time."

"That's about it. But did you effect a reconciliation with Joyce?"

"Only partly," said Simple. "A woman does not like to make up right away. They like to frown and pout so you will pet and beg 'em. But I do not beg nobody."

"What's your method, friend?"

"I leave—till they calm down, daddy-o. Just leave the house and let 'em cool off, put a little distance between troubles and me. Facts, I intend to put several days between myself and Joyce."

"You are not going by there and eat on Sunday as usual?"

"I can eat in Father's for Fifteen Cents—so why should I worry with Joyce?"

"Father Divine's is all very well. But his biscuits are nothing like Joyce's, that time she invited us to dinner last Easter."

"I do not care for biscuits when they are all mixed up with Who-Struck-John. Joyce must think a man don't have no place else to go except to her house. There's plenty womens in this world. And tonight I am dressed up so I know I don't look like Zip. Lend me a nickel, boy."

"For what?"

"To phone, what you think? I want to see how Joyce talks this evening. If she answers with one of them sweet *Hello's,* then changes her voice to a gravel bass when she finds out it's me, I will know she's still got her habits on."

"I thought you said just now you weren't going around there tonight."

"I'm *not* going, no matter how sweet she talks. But what

is a nickel? I would just juke-box it away on a record by Duke, so I might as well waste it on Joyce."

"You will want that nickel when times get hard."

"That's right," said Simple. "If this depression-recession gets any worse, *both* of us might want some of her biscuits, huh?"

"You have more foresight than I thought," I said. "Here's a nickel. Go call her up."

30

Equality and Dogs

"Even a black dog gets along better than me," mused Simple. "I have discovered that much since I been up North with these *liberal* white folks. You take this here social equality that some of them is always bringing up. I don't understand it. White folks socialize with dogs—yet they don't want to socialize with me."

"True," I said.

"White dogs, black dogs, any kind of dogs," Simple went on. "They don't care what color a dog is in New York. Why, when I first got here I used to drive for a woman out on Long Island who were so rich she had six dogs. One of 'em, a big black dog, slept in bed with her —right in bed with his rusty back up next to her white feet. But if a Negro set down six tables away from her in a restaurant, she almost had a fit. I do not understand it."

"You see plenty of dogs walking with white ladies on Park Avenue," I said.

"But no Negroes."

"That's right."

"They walk dogs and *work* Negroes," explained Simple. "While them rich white ladies is out walking with their dogs, Negroes are working back in their kitchens. Since the

34

The Law

"I definitely do not like the Law," said Simple, using the word with a capital letter to mean *police* and *courts* combined.

"Why?" I asked.

"Because the Law beats my head. Also because the Law will give a white man One Year and give me Ten."

"But if it wasn't for the Law," I said, "you would not have any protection."

"Protection?" yelled Simple. "The Law always protects a white man. But if *I* holler for the Law, the Law says, 'What do you want, Negro?' Only most white polices do not say 'Negro.'"

"Oh, I see. You are talking about the police, not the Law in general."

"Yes, I am talking about the polices."

"You have a bad opinion of the Law," I said.

"The Law has a bad opinion of me," said Simple. "The Law thinks *all* Negroes are in the criminal class. The Law'll stop me on the streets and shake me down—me, a workingman—as quick as they will any old weedheaded hustler or two-bit rounder. I do not like polices."

"You must be talking about the way-down-home-in-Dixie Law," I said, "not up North."

"I am talking about the Law *all over* America," said Simple, "North or South. In so far as I am concerned, a police is no good. It was the Law that started the Harlem riots by shooting that soldier-boy. Take a cracker down South or an o'fay up North—as soon as he puts on a badge he wants to try out his billy-club on some Negro's head. I tell you police are no good! If they was, they wouldn't be polices."

"Listen," I said, "you are generalizing too much. Not all cops are bad. There are some decent policemen—particularly in New York. You yourself told me about that good Irish cop downtown who made an insistent Southerner get out of a Negro's cab."

"I admit since the riots the cops ain't so bad in Harlem, and downtown there are some right nice ones. But outside of New York, you can count the good polices on the fingers of one glove," said Simple. "They are in the minorality."

"You mean *minority*. But what about the colored cops?" I asked. "Not all cops are white."

"Man!" said Simple, "colored cops are *colored,* so they can't bully *nobody* but me—which makes it worse. You know colored cops ain't gonna hit no white man. So when the black Law does get a chance to hit somebody once, they have to hit me *twice*. Colored cops is worse than white. A black Law is terrible!"

"I do not agree with you," I said. "I think there ought to be more colored cops."

"You can add, can't you?" asked Simple.

"Yes."

"Then use your rithematics. A black Law cannot lock up a white man in most cities, and he better not try. So when a colored cop does some arresting he has to lock up *two* or *three* of *me* to fill his quota—otherwise he never would get promoted."

"Well, anyhow, if it wasn't for the police, who would keep you from being robbed and mugged?"

"I have been robbed and mugged both," said Simple, "and there was not a cop nowhere to be found. I could not even find a P.D. car."

"Did you report being robbed?"

"I did the first time, but not no more. Them polices down at the precinct station looked at me like *I* were the robber. They asked me for all kinds of identifications from my driving license to my draft card. That was during the war. I told them, 'How can I show you my draft card when it was in my pocketbook and my pocketbook is just stole?' They wanted to lock me up for having no draft card."

"That does not sound plausible," I said.

"It may not sound possible—but it was," said Simple. "I told the Desk Sergeant that them mugs taken Eighty Dollars off of me at the point of a gun. The Desk Sergeant asked me *where did I get Eighty Dollars!* I showed him my hands. I said, 'See these here calluses? I work for my money,' I said. 'I do not graft, neither do I steal.'

"The Desk Sergeant hollered, 'Don't get smart, boy, or I'll throw *you* in the jug!' That is why I would not go back to no police station to report *nothing* no more."

"Maybe you'll be better treated next time."

"Not as long as I am black," said Simple.

"You look at everything, I regret to say, in terms of black and white."

"So does the Law," said Simple.

35

Confused

"When a Jew changes his name, he stops being Jewish, but I would have to change my color to stop being colored."

"True," I said. "Nature has got us fixed so we can't do a thing."

"Nature has got me in the go-long," said Simple. "No matter what I do, I am still black. I cannot pass for another nation, even if I change my name to Ahboo Ben Anklebar and wear a goatee."

"But being a race man," I said, "I know you are proud of being black."

"Proud as I can be," said Simple. "But sometimes it is mighty inconvenient. I remember once I was driving down South. I got the stomach-ache, but every service-station toilet on the road was marked WHITE. Every time I went near one, they hollered at me like a dog. Lord, I never will forget that! They tell me there are some hotels marked RESTRICTED into which a Jew cannot go. But I have never seen a toilet marked FOR CHRISTIANS ONLY."

"Neither have I," I said. "Besides, it is not so easy to tell with the eye who is a Jew and who is not."

"But me," said Simple, "I am marked for life. I am a

Son of Ham from down in 'Bam—and there ain't none
other like I am. Solid black from front to back! And one
thing sure—it won't fade, jack! The name I take makes
no difference either. I have known Negroes named
O'Malley, but they wasn't Irish. Anyhow, sometimes if
you get your name *too* white, it makes the white folks mad.
My second cousin on my stepuncle's side down in Virginia
named her first child Franklin D. Roosevelt Brown. But
the white folks she worked for told her, 'Mattie Mae, you
better take that white name off that black child. That's a
Yankee name, anyhow. In fact, a damn-yankee name.' "

"If you were going to pass for white, what name would
you take?" I asked.

"Patrick McGuire," said Simple.

"But why pick out an Irish name?"

"I don't know," said Simple, "I just like Irish names. If
I was going to pass for white, I might as well pass good.
With an Irish name, I could be Mayor of New York."

"A fine Mayor you would make."

"A fine Mayor is right," said Simple proudly. "I would
immediately issue a decree right away."

"To what effect?"

"To the effect that any colored man who wants to rent
an apartment downtown can rent one and no landlord can
tell him, 'We do not lease to colored.' "

"Always bringing in race," I said, "even after you get to
be Mayor."

"I would decree a landlord has to rent a house to anybody," said Simple. "I would not allow him to discriminate
against colored."

"Remember, now, this is all in case you would be white,"

I reminded him. "However, if you were white, sir, listen —would you want your daughter to marry a Negro?"

"If my daughter didn't have no better sense," said Simple.

"There you go showing prejudice yourself," I said.

"You got me confused, man! What I meant was . . ."

"Intermarriage is always brought up to confuse the issue," I said, "so don't bother to explain."

"Well, don't confuse *me!*" objected Simple. "In the first place, I am not white. In the second place, I don't have no daughter. And in the third place, if I did have, she wouldn't be white since I'm just passing for Irish myself. So don't confuse the issue. We was having a nice simple argument and you had to go confuse the issue. Buy me a beer."

"You drink too much," I said.

"Please don't confuse *another* issue," said Simple.

36

Something to Lean On

"A bar is something to lean on," said Simple.

"You lean on bars very often," I remarked.

"I do," said Simple.

"Why?"

"Because everything else I lean on falls down," said Simple, "including my peoples, my wife, my boss, and me."

"How do you mean?"

"My peoples brought me into the world," said Simple, "but they didn't have no money to put me through school. When I were knee-high to a duck I had to go to work."

"That happens to a lot of kids," I said.

"Most particularly colored," said Simple. "And my wife, I couldn't depend on her. When the depression come and I was out of a job, Isabel were no prop to me. I could not lean on her."

"So you started to leaning on bars," I said.

"No," said Simple. "I were leaning on bars before I married. I started to leaning on bars soon as I got out of short pants."

"Perhaps if you belonged to the church you would have something stronger on which to lean."

"You mean lean on the Lord? Daddy-o, too many folks

are leaning on Him now. I believe the Lord helps them that helps themselves—and I am a man who tries to help himself. That is the way white folks got way up where they are in the world—while colored's been leaning on the Lord."

"And you have been leaning on bars."

"What do you think I do all day long?" Simple objected. "From eight in the morning to five at night, I do not lean on no bar. I work! Ask my boss-man out at the plant. He knows I work. He claims he likes me, too. But that raise he promised me way last winter, have I got it yet? Also that advancement? No! I have not! I see them white boys get advancements while I stay where I am. Black—so I know I ain't due to go but so far. I bet you if I was white I would be somewhere in this world."

"There you go with that old color argument as an excuse again," I said.

"I bet you I would not be poor. All the opportunities a white man's got, there ain't no sense in his being poor. He can get any kind of job, anywhere. He can be President. Can I?"

"Do you have the qualifications?"

"Answer my question," said Simple, "and don't ask me another one. Can I be President? Truman can, but can I? Is he any smarter than me?"

"I am not acquainted with Mr. Truman, so I do not know."

"Does he *look* any smarter?" asked Simple.

"I must admit he does not," I said.

"Then why can't I be President, too? **Because I am** colored, that's why."

"So you spend your evenings leaning on bars because you cannot be President," I said. "What kind of reasoning is that?"

"Reason enough," said Simple. "If anybody else in America can be President, I want to be President. The Constitution guarantees us equal rights, but have I got 'em? No. It's fell down on me."

"You figure the Constitution has fallen down on you?"

"I do," said Simple. "Just like it fell down on that poor Negro lynched last month. Did anybody out of that mob go to jail? Not a living soul! But just kidnap some little small white baby and take it across the street, and you will do twenty years. The F.B.I. will spread its dragnet and drag in forty suspections before morning. And, if you are colored, don't be caught selling a half pint of bootleg licker, or writing a few numbers. They will put you in every jail there is! But Southerners can beat you, burn you, lynch you, and hang you to a tree—and every one of them will go scotfree. Gimme another beer. Tony! I can lean on this bar, but I ain't got another thing in the U.S.A. on which to lean."

PART FOUR

Any Time

37

In the Dark

"What you know, daddy-o?" hailed Simple.

"Where have you been so long lately?" I demanded.

"Chicago on my last two War Bonds," answered Simple, "to see my Cousin Art's new baby to which I am godfather —against his wife's will, because she is holy and sanctified."

"What is the trend of affairs in Chicago?" I inquired.

"Balling and brawling," said Simple. "And me with 'em."

"Did you take in the DeLisa?"

"No, I did not take in the DeLisa," said Simple, "but I went to the Brass Rail, also Square's, also that club on 63rd and South Park which jumps out loud. Also the Blue Dahlia."

"You got around, then."

"Sure did! I went to a couple of them new cocktail lounges, too, what don't have no light in 'em at all hardly. Chicago has the darkest bars in the world. So dark it is just like walking into a movie. Man, you have to stop and pause till you can see the bar. The booths are like Lovers' Lane, man. I thought my eyesight was failing the first time I went in one. Everything's the same color under them lightless lights. Ain't no telling whiskey from gin with the natural eye."

"You were probably intoxicated," I said.

"I was expecting to get high," said Simple, "but I did not succeed. The glass was thick that night and the whiskey thin. But I met a old chick who looked *fine* setting there in the dark, although I couldn't of seen her had she not had on a white hat. I asked her what her name was and she told me Bea.

" 'But don't get me wrong, King Kong, because I told you my name,' she said, 'I am a lady! My mama calls me Bea-Baby at home.'

"I said, 'What does your daddy call you?'

"She said, 'I has no daddy.'

"I said, 'You must be looking for *me* then.'

"She said, 'I *heard* you before I saw you so I could not have been *looking* for you. You abstract attention to yourself. But since you asked me, I drink Scotch.'

"So I ordered her some Teacher's. But that girl was thirsty! She drunk me up—at Sixty-Five Cents a shot! I said, 'Bea-Baby, let's get some air.'

"She said, 'Air? I growed up in air! I got plenty of air when I were a child. Sixteen miles south of Selma there weren't nothing but air.'

" 'Selma is far enough South, but *sixteen miles south of there* is too much! How long you been up North, girl?'

" 'Two years,' she said, 'and if I live to be a hundred, I will be up here seventy-five more.'

" 'You mean you are not going back to Selma?'

" 'Period,' she said.

" 'In other words, you are going to stay in Chicago?'

" 'Oh, but I am,' she said.

" 'Well, we are not going to stay in this bar seventy-five years,' I whispered. 'Come on, Bea-Baby, let's walk.'

" 'Walk where?' she hollered, insulted.

" 'Follow me and you will see,' I said.

" 'I will not follow you, unless you tell me where we are going.'

" 'I will not tell you where we are going, unless you follow,' I said.

"But when we got out of that darker-than-a-movie bar, under the street lights on Indiana Avenue, I got a good look at her and she got a good look at me. We *both* said 'Good-by!' In that dim dark old dusky cocktail lounge, I thought she was mellow. But she were not! I thought she was a chippy, but she were at least forty-five.

"And the first thing she said when she saw my face was, 'I thought you was a *young* man—but you ain't. You old as my Uncle Herman.'

"I said, 'I done had so many unpleasant surprises in my life, baby, until my age is writ in my face. *You* is one more unpleasantness.'

"I thought she said 'Farewell,' but it could of been 'Go to hell.'

"Anyhow, she cured me of them dark Chicago bars. *Never make friends in the dark,* is what I learned in Chicago."

"I am glad you learned something," I said.

"Thank you," said Simple. "Now, come on let's have a beer to welcome me back to Harlem. Not to change the subject, but lend me a quarter. I'm broke."

"I'm broke, too."

"Then you can't have a beer, daddy-o," regretted Simple. "What is worse, neither can I."

days of defense workers are long gone, that's where we are
again. Them rich white folks gave their big old yard dogs
they didn't like much to the army during the war, you
remember? The army trained 'em to fight just like a man.
But the army mostly trained Negroes to work—Quarter-
masters, Engineers, Port Battalions, Seabees. . . ."

"Yes."

"Um-hum-m-m! But they trained dogs to fight. Why, I
saw a picture of a dog getting a medal hung on his chest
for fighting so good he tore down a German machine-gun
nest. It were in a Southern white paper where I never
did see a picture of a Negro soldier getting a medal on his
chest. Every time them Southern papers had pictures of
Negroes in uniforms during the war, they was always un-
loading some landing barge or digging on some road. A
dog got a better break in the army than a Negro."

"You sound kind of bitter," I said, "about your army."

"How do you figger it's *my* army?" asked Simple as he
set his beer glass down.

"You pay taxes for it," I said.

"I do," said Simple, "but it pays me no mind. It Jim
Crows me, but it don't Jim Crow dogs. White dogs and
black dogs all served together in the army, didn't they?
And they didn't have no separate companies for black
dogs."

"You've got something there," I said.

"Come another war, I had rather be a dog in the army
any time than colored—especially down South. Why, I
saw in the newsreels once where they trained army dogs
to leap at a man and tear him down—to leap at a *white*
man, at that. But if I even as much as raise a hand at a

cracker when he pushes me off the sidewalk, my head is beat and I am put in jail. But a dog in the army, they taught him not to let nobody push him off no sidewalk in Mississippi nor nowhere else. Here I am a human, and I get less of a break in the U.S. than a dog! I do not understand."

"Neither do I," I said.

"How come you ain't arguing with me tonight?" asked Simple. "You mighty near always disagree."

"How can I disagree about dogs?" I said.

"I remember in the first depression times before the war, when they had the WPA and the PWA and all those things that it was so hard to get on, and that you got so little from after you did get on 'em. I remember seeing folks come into meat markets and buy great big pieces of good red meat for their dogs, while plenty colored folks, and white, too, didn't have meat for themselves and their children. I said to myself then that it must be good to be a dog. I said, eating *fine* red meat and not having to worry about getting on WPA. Black dogs and white dogs all eating good red meat and no color line between 'em. I tell you, dogs rate better in America than colored folks."

"Anyhow, I love dogs," I said, "and I'm glad they get a break in our paradoxical society."

"I love dogs, too," said Simple, "but I love colored folks better."

"Still you want to take the meat out of a dog's mouth."

"I do not," said Simple. "I just want some meat in my own mouth, that's all! I want the same chance a dog has. Furthermore, I do not care to argue about it. Doggone if I'm going to argue about dogs!"

31

Seeing Double

"I wonder why it is we have two of one thing, and only one of others."

"For instance?"

"We have two lungs," said Simple, "but only one heart. Two eyes, but only one mouth. Two——"

"Feet, but only one body," I said.

"I was not going to say *feet*," said Simple. "But since you have taken the words out of my mouth, go ahead."

"Human beings have two shoulders but only one neck."

"And two ears but only one head," said Simple.

"What on earth would you want with two heads?"

"I could sleep with one and stay awake with the other," explained Simple. "Just like I got two nostrils, I would also like to have two mouths, then I could eat with one mouth while I am talking with the other. Joyce always starts an argument while we are eating, anyhow. That Joyce can talk and eat all at once."

"Suppose Joyce had two mouths, too," I said. "She could double-talk you."

"I would not keep company with a woman that had two mouths," said Simple. "But I would like to have two myself."

"If you had two mouths, you would have to have two noses also," I said, "and it would not make much sense to have two noses, would it?"

"No," said Simple, "I reckon it wouldn't. Neither would I like to have two chins to have to shave. A chin is no use for a thing. But there is one thing I sure would like to have two of. Since I have—"

"Since you have two eyes, I know you would like to have two faces—one in front and one behind—so you could look at all those pretty women on the street both going and coming."

"That would be idealistic," said Simple, "but that is *not* what I was going to say. You always cut me off. So you go ahead and talk."

"I know you wish you had two stomachs," I said, "so you could eat more of Joyce's good cooking."

"No, I do *not* wish I had two stomachs," said Simple. "I can put away enough food in one belly to mighty near wreck my pocketbook—with prices as high as a cat's back in a dogfight. So I do not need two stomachs. Neither do I need two navels on the stomach I got. What use are they? But there is one thing I sure wish I had two of."

"Two gullets?" I asked.

"Two gullets is *not* what I wish I had at all," said Simple. "Let me talk! *I wish I had two brains.*"

"Two brains! Why?"

"So I could think with one, and let the other one rest, man, that's why. I am tired of trying to figure out how to get ahead in this world. If I had two brains, I could think with one brain while the other brain was asleep. I could plan with one while the other brain was drunk. I could think about the Dodgers with one, and my future with the other. As it is now, there is too much in this world for one brain to take care of alone. I have thought so much with my one brain that it is about wore out. In fact, I need a rest right now. So let's drink up and talk about something pleasant. Two beers are on me tonight. Draw up to the bar."

"I was just at the bar," I said, "and Tony has nothing but bottles tonight, no draft."

"Then, daddy-o, they're on *you*," said Simple. "I only got two dimes—and one of them is a Roosevelt dime I do not wish to spend. Had I been thinking, I would have remembered that Roosevelt dime. When I get my other brain, it will keep track of all such details."

32

Right Simple

"Once when I was a chauffeur and yard-man, also relief butler, for that rich old country white lady down in Virginia, she kept me working twenty-five hours a day. She could find something for me to do *all* the time."

"Well, at least, it kept you out of mischief," I commented.

"I still had time to get in trouble," said Simple. "She had a pretty upstairs maid named Polly Joe who were married—but she had been married long enough to get used to her husband. At that time, I were a young boy, sharp, also good-looking—which you might not think to see me now, although there is still something about me womens fall for. Anyhow, I played her cool. I did not let Polly Joe know why I had to come upstairs so often when I should have been polishing the silver or the car. I come near polishing the backs right off of that old white lady's silver comb and brush set just so I could get to set and talk on them upper floors to Polly Joe. And it looked like the more I looked at that girl, the more I wanted to taste some of her lipstick.

"Now, somebody went and told Polly's husband. You know, it is a shame some nice womens is married to such

mean husbands. Her husband did not like me a-tall. I were
younger than him. He was a deacon in the Zion Baptist
Church and did not gallivant. I did. So one evening I says
to Polly Joe, 'Honey, baby-girl, dear, I could take you
down the road a piece and show you what a juke-joint
looks like.'

"Polly Joe says, 'Somebody would be sure to tell my
husband if I went out with you.'

"I says, 'You could swear it was a lie, that you was right
here on your job that night sleeping in.'

"She says, 'Ain't you afraid of married womens?'

"I said, 'Are you afraid of a married man?'

"She said, 'No, I am just scared of my husband.'

"I said, 'Pay him no mind! He will be home in bed
while you and me will be down the road at Sy's listening
to that mellow treble and drinking mountain dew. It is
not good to work for white folks all day long and half the
night and not have no pleasure a-tall. You know that.'

"Polly Joe says, 'I sure do know! I believe I will go out
with you—just once. But don't let nobody know it. If my
husband——!'

" 'Baby, let's leave your husband out of this,' I said.

"Everything would have been all right had not the cook
got wind of it when Polly Joe went to borrow her gold earrings. It happened that of *all* the nights to telephone, that
was one night when Polly Joe's husband called up from in
town. He says, 'Where is Polly Joe?'

"Old fat cook says, 'She's gone to Sy's.'

" 'Sy who's?' said the husband.

" 'Sy's juke,' said the cook.

" 'My wife has got no business in that joint,' says the husband, 'and me a pillar of Zion Baptist Church!'

" 'She's in good company,' says the cook.

" 'What company?' says the husband.

" 'Jess Semple's,' says the cook.

"Well, sir! That Negro mighty near tore that phone from the wall. He had heard from the womens what a man I am, so he got in his Ford and headed for Sy's Roadhouse. The cook said the language she heard on the phone was not from a Christian. She wondered how could a deacon know such words."

"Get on with the story," I said. "What happened to you that night?"

"I am ashamed to say," said Simple. "When the deacon walked in Sy's place I was dancing, holding Polly Joe closer than a hanger holds a suit. The music were so good I could not afford to move my feet for fear I might miss a beat. I did not know her husband was there until I felt something strike me where I didn't set down again for a week. It were his foot. I also felt something grab me by the collar. It were his hand. Then I felt somebody flying through the door. That were me. Something put a dent in the concrete highway. It were my head.

"Man, I *ran!* I *solid* ran! I did not touch the road, I ran in the air. When I looked back, I did not see Polly Joe neither her husband because I were two miles off. I run so fast I strained a linament in my ankle. Polly Joe's husband made her quit that job. The next maid our old mistress-lady hired were fifty-one years old. And it were a month before my head got back to normal and that knot resided. As many girls as I knowed when I were young, I didn't have to take no married woman out. Sometimes, you know, I think I am right simple."

33

Ways and Means

"You see this, don't you?" said Simple, showing me his N.A.A.C.P. card. "I have just joined the National Organization for the Association of Colored Folks and it is fine."

"You mean the National Association for the Advancement of Colored People," I said.

"Um-hum!" said Simple, "but they tell me it has white people in it, too."

"That's right, it does."

"I did not see none at the meeting where me and Joyce went this evening," said Simple.

"No?"

"No! There should have been some present because that *fine* colored speaker was getting white folks told—except that there was no white folks there to be told."

"They just do not come to Negro neighborhoods to meetings," I said, "although they may belong."

"Then we ought to hold some meetings downtown so that they can learn what this Negro problem is all about," said Simple. "It does not make sense to be always talking to ourselves. We know we got troubles. But every last Italian, Jew, and Greek what owns a business all up and

down Seventh Avenue and Eighth Avenue and Lenox in
Harlem ought to have been there. Do you reckon they belong to anything colored?"

"I don't expect they do," I said.

"Well, next time I go to a A.A.C.P. meeting . . ."

"N-A-A-C-P meeting," I said.

". . . N.A.A.C.P. meeting, I am going to move that
everybody get a coin can," said Simple, "and go from
store to store and bar to bar and hash-house to hash-house
and take up collection for the N.A.A.C.P., from all these
white folks making money in colored neighborhoods. If
they don't give, I will figure they do not care nothing about
my race. White folks are always taking up collections from
me for the Red· Cross or the Community Chest or the
Cancer Drive or the March of Dimes or something or
other. They are always shaking their cans in *my* face. Why
shouldn't I shake my can in *their* face?"

"It would be better," I said, "if you got them all to be
members of the N.A.A.C.P., not just to give a contribu-
tion."

"Every last white businessman in Harlem ought to belong to the N.A.A.C.P., but do you reckon they would ever
come to meetings? They practically all live in the suburbans."

"They come to Harlem on business," I said, "so why
shouldn't they come to the meetings?"

"That is why they go to the suburbans, to get away
from the Negroes they have been selling clothes and gro-
ceries and victuals and beer all day. They do not want to
be bothered with me when they close up their shops."

"Do you blame them?" I said.

"I do," said Simple. "Long as the cash register is ring-
ing, they can be bothered with me, so why can't they come
to an N.A.A.C.P. meeting?"

"Have I ever heard of you going out to the Italian or
Jewish or Irish neighborhoods to any of their meetings to
help them with their problems?" I asked.

"I do not have any stores in the Italian or Jewish
neighborhoods," said Simple. "Neither do I own nary
pool hall in an Irish neighborhood, nor nary Greek restaurant, nor nary white apartment house from which I get
rent. I do not own no beer halls where Jews and Italians
come to spend their money. If I did, I would join the
Jewish N.A.A.C.P., and the Italian one, too! I would also
join the Greek N.A.A.C.P., if I owned a hash-house where
nothing but Greeks spent money all day long like I spend
money in their Greasy Spoons."

"You put social co-operation on such a mercenary
basis," I said.

"They would want me to have mercy on them if they
was in my fix," said Simple.

"I did not say anything about mercy. I said *mercenary*
—I mean a buying-and-selling basis."

"They could buy and sell me," said Simple.

"What I mean is, you should not have to have a business in a Jewish neighborhood to be interested in Jewish
problems, or own a spaghetti stand to be interested in
Italians, or a bar to care about the Irish. In a democracy,
everybody's problems are related, and it's up to all of us
to help solve them."

"If I did not have a business reason to be interested in

their business," said Simple, "then what business would I have being interested in *their* business?"

"Just a human reason," I said. "It's all human business."

"Maybe that is why they don't join the N.A.A.C.P.," said Simple. "Because they do not think a Negro is human."

"If I were you, I would not speak so drastically unless I had some facts to go on. Have you ever asked any of the white businessmen where you trade to join the N.A.A.C.P. —the man who runs your laundry, or manages the movies where you go, or the Greek who owns the restaurant? Have you asked any of them to join?"

"No, I have not. Neither have I asked my colored landlady's white landlord."

"Well, ask them and see what they say."

"I sure will," said Simple, "then if they do not join, I will know they don't care nothing about me."

"You make it very simple," I said.

"It is simple, because everybody knew what stores to pick out the night of the riot."

"I was in Chicago that summer of '43 so I missed the riot."

"I was in it," said Simple.

"You don't say! Tell me about it. Where you that night?"

"All up and down," said Simple.

"Grabbing hams out of broken windows?"

"No," said Simple, "I did not want no ham. I wanted Justice."

"What do you mean, Justice?"

"You know what I mean," Simple answered. "That cop had no business shooting a colored soldier!"

"You had no business breaking up stores, either," I said. "That is no way to get Justice."

"That is the way the Allies got it—breaking up Germany, breaking up Hiroshima, and everything in sight. But these white folks are more scared of Negroes in the U.S.A. than they ever was of Hitler, otherwise why would they make Jackie Robinson stop playing baseball to come to Washington and testify how loyal we is? I remember that night after the riots they turned on all the street lights in Harlem, although it was during the war and New York had a dim-out. Wasn't no dim-out in Harlem —lights just blazing in the middle of the war. The air-raid drill was called off, likewise the blackout. Suppose them German planes had come with *all* our lights on full."

"You're so dark the cops couldn't see *you* in a dim-out so they had to turn on the lights."

"Make no remarks about my color, pal! You are the same complexion. And I'll bet if you'd been in New York when the riot started, you would have been out there in the streets with me."

"I would have emerged to see the excitement, yes, but not to break windows looking for Justice."

"Well, *I* was looking for Justice," said Simple. "I was tired."

"Tired of what?"

"Of hearing the radio talking about the Four Freedoms all day long during the war and me living in Harlem where nary one of them Freedoms worked—nor the ceiling prices neither."

"So?"

"So I threw a couple of bricks through a couple of windows when the riots started, and I felt better."

"Did you pick your windows or did you just throw?"

"Man, there wasn't no time to pick windows because the si-reens was blowing and the P.D.'s coming. But I aimed my foot at one grocery and my bricks at two big windows in a shoe store that cost them white folks plenty money to put back in."

"And that made you feel better?"

"Yes."

"Why?"

"Well, I figured, let them white men spend some of the profits they make out of Harlem putting those windows back. Let 'em spend some of that money they made out of these high rents in Harlem all these years to put them windows back. Also let 'em use some of that money to put them windows back that they owe my grandmother and my great-grandmother and her mother before that for working all them years in slavery for nothing. Let 'em take *that* back pay due my race and put them windows back!"

"You have things all mixed up, old man," I said, "which is one reason why I am glad you have joined the N.A.A.C. P., so that the next time a crisis comes up, you will have a more legitimate outlet for your energies. There are more effective ways and means of achieving justice than through violence. The N.A.A.C.P. believes in propaganda, education, political action, and legal redress. Besides, the men who owned that shoe store you threw those bricks in probably were way over in Europe when you were born.

Certainly they had nothing to do with slavery, let alone your grandma's back pay."

"But they don't have nothing to do now with *Grandma's grandson* either—except to take my money over the counter, then go on downtown to Stuyvesant Town where I can't live, or out to them pretty suburbans, and leave me in Harlem holding the bag. I ain't no fool. When the riot broke out, I went looking for Justice."

"With a brick."

"No! Two bricks," said Simple.

38

For the Sake of Argument

When I came out of the house about midnight to get a bite to eat, there was Simple in one corner of Paddy's Bar arguing loudly with an aggregation of beer-drinkers as to who is the darker, Paul Robeson or Jackie Robinson. I sat down on the lunch-counter side of the bar and ordered a plate of shortribs. After a while Simple spotted me and took possession of the next stool, although he had no apparent intention of eating.

"You know Robeson is not as light as Robinson," he announced.

"To me it makes not the slightest difference what their gradations of complexion are," I said. "Furthermore, I do not comprehend how you can stand around for hours in bars and on corners just arguing about nothing. You will argue with folks about which railroad has the fastest trains, or if Bojangles could tap more taps per second than Fred Astaire. And none of it is of any importance."

"I do not see how you can sit around looking so smart all the time and saying practically nothing," countered Simple. "You are company for nobody but yourself."

"I do not like to argue," I said.

"I do! I will argue about whether or not two and two makes four just for the sake of argument."

"It has been proven so long ago that two and two make four that I do not see the sense in discussing it. If you were arguing about what to do with the Germans or how to reform the South, then I could go along with you. But I do not like to argue about things on which there is really no argument."

"I do—because my argument is that it is good for a man to argue, just argue," said Simple, walking to the door of the bar and gazing out. Suddenly he turned around. "But I could not argue if you did not argue back at me. It takes two to make an argument. A man cannot argue by his self."

"The trouble with you is that you always wish to *win* the argument," I said. "For me, just an exchange of views is sufficient. But you, you always want to win."

"Naturally, I want to win. Otherwise, why should I be arguing?"

"You are so often wrong, Jess, also loud. You cannot win an argument when you are wrong. There are two sides to every question."

"There are sometimes more than two sides," said Simple, "except to the race question. For white folks that don't have but one side."

"There you go bringing up the race question," I said. "How is it two Negroes can never get together without discussing the race question?"

"Because it is not even a question," said Simple. "It is a hammer over our heads and at any time it may fall. The only way I can explain what white folks does to us is that they just don't give a damn. Why, I once knowed a white man down South who were so mean he wouldn't give a sick baby a doctor's address."

"Where and when was that?" I asked.

"When I were a boy," said Simple. "I was hired out one summer on his plantation. He used to ride all around over the plantation watching everybody work. He rid on a little old girl-horse named Betsy, and Betsy were as mean as he were. In fact, he had taught Betsy how to bite Negroes in the back. 'Boy, hist that there tree out of that ditch!'

"If you did not hist fast enough to suit him—'I can't, Capt'n Boss!'—he would holler, 'Boy, you better, else I'll bull-whip your hide wide open!'

"Then if you still didn't hist, he would tell that little old horse, 'Get him, Betsy!' Betsy would gallop up and nip you right between the shoulder blades."

"You are lying now, I do believe," I said.

"You have never lived down South," said Simple, "so you do not know."

"I admit I am not really familiar with the South," I said, "but sometimes I think conditions are exaggerated. Certainly in recent years they are getting better."

"They've still got Jim Crow cars," said Simple. "And the last time I was down home on a trip, I went to pay a visit on the old white man my uncle used to work for. I had kinder forgot how it is down there, so I just walked up on the porch where he was setting and says, 'Howdy, Mr. Doolittle.'

"He says, 'Boy, take off your hat when you address a white man.' And that is how he greeted me. He says, 'You

must have been up North so long you done forgot yourself.'

"You know that kinder hurt my feelings because he used
to know me when I was a boy. But I am a man now. That
is the trouble with the South. They do not want to treat a
Negro like a man. It's always *boy,* no matter if you are
ninety-nine years old. I know some few things is getting
better, but even them is slow as molasses. Here, lemme
show you a little poem I writ about that very thing last
week."

Simple pulled a piece of tablet paper out of his pocket
and proceeded to read. "Listen fluently:

> *Old Jim Crow's*
> *Just panting and a-coughing,*
> *But he won't take wings*
> *And fly.*
>
> *Old Jim Crow*
> *Is laying in his coffin,*
> *But he don't want*
> *To die.*
>
> *I have writ*
> *His obituary,*
> *Still and yet*
> *He tarry.*"

"Not bad, old man, except that 'He tarry' is not gram-
matical," I said. "If you want to be literary, you ought to
know grammar."

"Joyce knows grammar," said Simple. "She will fix it
up for me. I just have not showed her this one yet."

"A writer should never depend on anyone else to fix things for him. You ought to fix up your own things," I said.

"There are some things in life you cannot fix all by yourself," said Simple. "For me, poetries is one. And the race problem is another. Now you take for instant, we got two colored congressmen down in Washington. But they can't even stop a filibuster. Every time them Civil Rights Bills come up, them old white Southerners filibuster them to hell and gone. Why don't them colored congressmen start a filibuster, too?"

"Probably because they cannot talk as long or as loud as the Southerners," I said. "It takes Southerners to keep a filibuster going, and there are a great many of them in the House. Neither Adam Powell nor Dawson represents the South."

"They are colored and they represent me," said Simple. "If I was down yonder in Congress representing the colored race, I would start a filibuster all my own. In fact, I would filibuster to keep them filibusters from starting a filibuster."

"If you had no help," I said, "you would just have to keep on talking day and night, week after week, because once you sat down somebody else would get the floor. So how would you hold out?"

"How would I hold out?" yelled Simple. "With the fate of my Race at stake, you ask me how would *I* hold out! Why, for my people I would talk until my tongue hung out of my mouth. I would talk until I could not talk no more! Then, I would use sign language. When I got through with that, I would get down on my knees and pray in silence. And nobody better not strike no gavel while I am communing with my Maker. While I am on my knees, I would get some sleep. When I riz up, it would be the next day, so I would start all over again. I would be the greatest one-man filibuster of all time, daddy-o! But I am running dry now. Treat me to a beer."

"I will not," I said.

"O.K., then," said Simple, "you are setting there eating and drinking and here I am empty-handed. You are a hell of a buddy."

"I will lend you a dime to buy your own beer," I said, "but a treat should be an invitation, not a request."

"Just so I get the beer," said Simple. "Now, I will continue. As I were saying, there ain't but one side to this race question—the white folks' side. White folks are setting on top of the world, and I wouldn't mind setting up there myself. Just look around you. Who owns this bar? White folks. Who owns mighty near every shop and store all up and down this street? White folks. But what do I own? I'm asking you."

"As far as I know, you do not own a thing. But why don't you get a bar or a store?"

"Why don't you?"

"Let's consider the broader picture," I said.

"I asked you a question," said Simple. "Why don't *you* get a bar or a store?"

"I asked you first," I countered.

"I do not get a bar or a store for the same reason that you don't," said Simple. "I have nothing to get me one with. On Saturday I draws my wages. I pay my rent, I get out my laundry, I take Joyce to a show, I pay you back your Two Dollars, I drink a little beer. What have I got left to buy a store with?"

"Do you think Tony the Italian that owns this Paddy's Bar—with its Irish name—also two stores, and a bookie joint, had anything when he came to America twenty years ago in the steerage?"

"Columbus come before him and smoothed the way," said Simple. "Besides, if you are white, you can get credit. If you are white, you can meet somebody with money. If you are white, you can come up here to Harlem and charge double prices. If I owned a store and charged what they charge, folks would say, 'That Negro is no good.' I tell you, white folks get away with murder. They murder my soul every day and my pocketbook every night. They got me going and coming. They say, 'You can't have a good job. You're black.' Then they say, 'Pay double. You can't eat downtown. We got this grease-ball joint for you in Harlem where it's a dime more for a beef stew. Pay it or else!' A man can't else. That's the way they get ahead when they come to America. Columbus didn't start out with Jim Crow around his neck. Neither did the guy who owns this bar. Any foreigner can come here, white, and Jim Crow me, black, from the day he sets foot off the boat. Also overcharge. He *starts* on top of my head so no wonder he gets on top of the world. Maybe I ought to go to Europe and come back a foreigner."

"While you are over there, in order to change your complexion, you'd have to be born again."

"As colored as I am," said Simple, "I'd have to be born two or three times."

39

Simple Pins On Medals

"Now, the way I understand it," said Simple one Monday evening when the bar was nearly empty and the juke box silent, "it's been written down a long time ago that all men are borned equal and everybody is entitled to life and liberty while pursuing happiness. It's in the Constitution, also Declaration of Independence, so I do not see why it has to be resolved all over again."

"Who is resolving it all over?" I asked.

"Some white church convention—I read in the papers where they have resolved all that over and the Golden Rule, too, also that Negroes should be treated right. It looks like to me white folks better stop resolving and get to *doing*. They have resolved enough. *Resolving ain't solving.*"

"What do you propose that they do?"

"The white race has got a double duty to us," said Simple. "They ought to start treating us right. They also ought to make up for how bad they have treated us in the past."

"You can't blame anybody for history," I said.

"No," said Simple, "but you can blame folks if they don't do something about history! History was yesterday, times gone. Yes. But now that colored folks are willing to let bygones be bygones, this ain't no time to be Jim Crowing nobody. This is a new day."

"Maybe that is why they are resolving to do better," I said.

"I keep telling you, it has come time to stop *resolving!*" said Simple. "They have been *resolving* for two hundred years. I do not see how come they need to *resolve* any more. I say, they need to *solve.*"

"How?"

"By treating us like humans," said Simple, "that's how!"

"They don't treat each other like human beings," I said, "so how do you expect them to treat you that way?"

"White folks do not Jim Crow each other," said Simple, "neither do they have a segregated army—except for me."

"No, maybe not," I said, "but they blasted each other down with V-bombs during the war."

"To be shot down is bad for the body," said Simple, "but to be Jim Crowed is worse for the spirit. Besides, speaking of war, in the next war I want to see Negroes pinning medals on white men."

"Medals? What have medals to do with anything?"

"A lot," said Simple, "because every time I saw a picture in the colored papers of colored soldiers receiving medals in the last war, a white officer was always doing the pinning. I have not yet seen a picture in *no* papers of a *colored* officer pinning a medal on a white soldier. Do you reckon I will ever see such a picture?"

"I don't know anything about the army's system of pinning on medals," I said.

"I'll bet there isn't a white soldier living who ever got a medal from a colored officer," said Simple.

"Maybe not, but I don't get your point. If a soldier is brave enough to get a medal, what does it matter who pins it on?"

"It may not matter to the soldiers," said Simple, "but it matters to *me*. I have never yet seen no *colored* general pinning a medal on a *white* private. That is what I want to see."

"Colored generals did not command white soldiers in the last war," I said, "which is no doubt why they didn't pin medals on them."

"I want to see colored generals commanding white soldiers, then," said Simple.

"You may want to see it, but how can you see it when it just does not take place?"

"In the next war it must and should take place," said Simple, "because if these white folks are gonna have another war, they better give us some generals. I know if I was in the army, I would like to command white troops. In fact, I would like to be in charge of a regiment from Mississippi."

"Are you sober?" I asked.

"I haven't had but one drink today."

"Then why on earth would you want to be in charge of a white regiment from Mississippi?"

"They had white officers from Mississippi in charge of Negroes—so why shouldn't I be in charge of whites? Huh? I would really make 'em toe the line! I know some of them Southerners had rather die than to *left face* for a colored man, buddy-o. But they would *left face* for me."

"What would you do if they wouldn't *left face?*"

"Court-martial them," said Simple. "After they had set in the stockade for six months, I would bring them Mississippi white boys out, and I would say once more, *'Left face!'* I bet they would *left face* then! Else I'd court-martial them again."

"You have a very good imagination," I said, "also a sadistic one."

"I can see myself now in World War III," said Simple, "leading my Mississippi troops into action. I would do like all the other generals do, and stand way back on a hill somewheres and look through my spyglasses and say, 'Charge on! Mens, charge on!' Then I would watch them Dixiecrat boys go—like true sons of the old South, mowing down the enemy.

"When my young white lieutenants from Vicksburg jeeped back to Headquarters to deliver their reports in person to me, they would say, 'General Captain, sir, we have taken two more enemy positions.'

"I would say, 'Mens, return to your companies—and tell 'em to *charge on!'*

"Next day, when I caught up to 'em, I would pin medals on their chests for bravery. Then I would have my picture taken in front of all my fine white troops—*me*—the first black American general to pin medals on white soldiers from Mississippi. It would be in every paper in the world —the great news event of World War III."

"It would certainly be news," I said.

"Doggone if it wouldn't," said Simple. "It would really be news! You see what I mean by *solving*—not just re-solving. I will've done solved."

40

A Ball of String

"This makes me mad." My friend frowned as he came back to his stool from the telephone booth at the rear of the bar. "I do not like Zarita nor no other dame calling me up at a bar, having the bartender strewing my right and full name all over the place, 'Hey, there, Jesse B. Semple! One of your womens wants you on the phone. But she's way down at the end of the alphabet—Z, for Zarita.' That bartender ain't got no business letting everybody know my business and I don't care to have my name known to everybody, neither."

"He is not very discreet," I said, "but then, Harlemites have very little training in public service, since they don't get a chance to acquire background in business elsewhere."

"Bartenders are most in generally all right," said Simple, "but some of these waitresses get me down—unless they are damn good-looking. Also some Harlem clerks don't know how to wait on people. The other day I went in a Dime store on 125th Street. Young girl clerk was standing back behind the counter chewing gum and looking like a baby bull moose. I asked for a Ten-Cent ball of string.

" 'I don't have none,' she snaps.

"I said, 'Do you mean to tell me you don't have a Ten-

Cent ball of string in all this great big old Dime store?"

" 'It costs *Twelve* Cents,' she said.

"Why didn't you tell me that in the first place?' I asked her. 'All I want is what *used* to be a Ten-Cent ball of' string. I do not care if it costs Twelve Cents now or not. I need the string.'

"Whereupon she grabs a ball of twine, throws it in a bag, and throws it at me. Now I do not very seldom get mad, daddy-o, but I got mad this time. That girl were colored like me and ought to treat *me* with some politeness. So I says, 'Young lady, look here! If you stop chewing gum long enough to let your ears stay in one place and hear what I have to say, I will tell you something. Do you remember when they did not let any colored clerks work in these white stores here in Harlem? Huh? Do you? Well, I was one of the mens that picketed in the snow in my bare shoes with no overshoes to get you-all these jobs. Now I will picket *to get you out again,* if you do not give me some kind of decent service.'

" 'I give you what you wanted,' she snaps. 'That is the trouble with colored folks, they always expect more out of us than they do out of white clerks. You've got your string.'

" 'Yes, I've got my string,' I said, 'but I would not have had it had I listened to you in the first place, telling me, Naw, you didn't have any, when what you should have said was, Yes, we have it, but the price is gone up to Twelve Cents—even if this is a Dime store. I cannot figure out why colored clerks say "No" so much.'

" 'You should ask for what you want,' said the girl, lowering her head at me and chewing like a young cow.

" 'I did ask for what I want—string,' I said. 'But I am no clerk, so how do I know to ask for *Twelve-Cent* string when it used to be Ten? Don't pull no teck on me, young lady, and me as black as you.'

" 'You talk like you've never been mistreated by no white clerks in a store,' she says.

" 'That is just why I picketed to get colored clerks in this store,' I says, 'so I wouldn't be snipped up and ignored. Now here you come telling me, Naw, you don't have no string, when you do. Then getting technical about Two Cents' difference in the price. I got a good mind to report you to the manager.'

" 'That's what I say about Negroes—always running to the white man,' said the young woman. 'What do you want, madam?' she says to a large lady who has been waiting all this time.

" 'A box of sealing wax,' said the woman.

" 'That is not at this counter,' snaps the girl, so the woman wandered on off looking all around to see if she could see any sealing wax laying loose somewhere.

"I said, 'Why didn't you tell that woman where the sealing wax is?'

"She says, 'Because I don't know, that's why! I'm not supposed to know where everything in this store is.'

" 'If you knew a little more, you might get a little further,' I said. '*No! I don't know! No! I don't have! No! No, ma'am! No!* Sometimes I think all you clerks know is *No!* Is that so?'

" 'No,' she snaps, 'it's not so! No!'

"Then I says, 'Tell me then where the shoe-polish counter is.'

"She says, 'I think it's in the rear.'

" 'You think?' I says. 'Then you do not know? How long have you been working here?'

" 'Four years and none of your business,' she says.

" 'Then I should think you would know where *something* is in this store,' I said.

" 'Stop heckling me!' she said.

" 'I heckled to get you in here,' I said.

"About that time a young slick-headed dude come up and says, 'Say, baby, how you doing? What time you gonna be ready to cut out of this joint and run by Slim's and Mary's with me, huh?'

"She says, 'Daddy, you know I told you I'm not going around to Mary's any more after she talked about me like a dog.'

"I said, 'Young lady, do you realize you still got a customer?'

"She says, 'Where?'

"I said, 'Don't you consider me a customer?'

"She says, 'No—because you got your string.'

"I said, 'I got my string—but I don't have satisfaction.'

"She says, 'We don't sell that at this counter.'

"Whereupon that young cat what didn't even work there hollers, 'Are you trying to insult my girl friend?' ·

"Buddy-o, what I said to him will not bear repeating! Me and that cat would have tangled right in that Twelve-Cent Dime store if not an old lady had come up and said, 'Now, sons, sons, you-all are acting just like Negroes.' That made me ashamed, so I cut out."

"Were you acting like a Negro?" I asked.

"I was acting like myself," said Simple.

41

Blue Evening

When I walked into the bar and saw him on the corner stool alone, I could tell something was wrong.

"Another hang-over?"

"Nothing that simple. This is something I thought never would happen to me."

"What?" I asked.

"That a woman could put *me* down. In the past, I have always left womens. No woman never left me. Now Joyce has quit."

"I don't believe it," I said. "You've been going together for two or three years, and getting along fine. What happened? That little matter of the divorce from your wife, the fur coat, or what?"

"Zarita," said Simple.

"Zarita! She's nothing to you."

"I know it," said Simple. "She never was nothing to me but a now-and-then. But Zarita has ruint my life. You don't know how it feels, buddy, when somebody has gone that you never had before. I never had a woman like Joyce. I *loved* that girl. Nobody never cared for me like Joyce did."

"Have a drink," I said, "on me."

"This is one time I do not want a drink. I feel too bad."

"Then it *is* serious," I said.

"It's what the blues is made out of," said Simple. " 'Love, oh, love, oh, careless love!' Buddy, I were careless."

"What happened, old man?"

"Zarita," said Simple. "I told that woman never to come around to my room without letting me know in advance. Joyce is too much of a lady to be always running up to my place, which is why I love her. Only time Joyce might ring my bell is when she can't get me on the phone due to my landlady is evil and sometimes will not even deliver a message. Then maybe Joyce might ring my bell, but she never comes upstairs, less it is to hang me some new spring curtains she made herself or change my dresser scarf. What's come up now is Zarita's fault, plus my landlady's. Them two womens is against me. That word *Town & Country* uses for female dogs just about fits them."

"I understand. They are not genteel characters. But what exactly took place?"

"It hurts me to think of it, let alone to talk about it. But I will tell you. Zarita not only came around to my room the other night, but she brought her whole birthday party *unannounced, uninvited,* and *unwanted.* I didn't even know it were her birthday. I had just come in from work, et a little supper at the Barbecue Shack, and was preparing to take a nap to maybe go out later and drop by to see were Joyce in the mood, when my doorbell rung like mad nine times—which is the ring for my Third Floor Rear. It were about nine P.M. I go running downstairs in my shirttail, and sixty-eleven Negroes, male and female, come pouring in the door led by Zarita herself, whooping and hollering and high, yelling they come to help me celebrate her birthday, waving three or four bottles of licker and gin.

"Zarita says, 'Honey, I forgot to tell you I'm twenty-some-odd years old today. Whoopeee-eee-e! We started celebrating this morning and we still going strong. Come on up, folks! Let's play his combination. This man has got some *fine* records!'

"I didn't have a chance to say nothing. They just poured up the steps with me trailing behind, and my landlady looking cross-eyed out of her door, and Zarita talking so loud you could hear her in Buffalo. Next thing I knowed, Louis Jordan was turned up full-blast and somebody had even put a loud needle in the victrola. Them Negroes took possession. Well, you know I always tries to be a gentleman, even to Zarita, so I did not ask them out. I just poured myself a half glass of gin—which I do not ordinarily partake. Then I hollered, 'Happy birthday,' too.

"Well, the rest of the roomers heard the function and started coming in my room. Boyd next door brought his girl friend over, and before you knowed it, the ball was on. The joint jumped! To tell the truth, I even enjoyed myself.

"By and by, Zarita said, 'Honey, send out and get some more to drink.'

" 'Send who?' I said. 'We ain't got no messenger boy.'

"She said, 'Just gimme the money, then, and I will send that old down-home shmoo who has been trying to make love to me since four o'clock this afternoon. That man ain't nothing to me but a errand boy.'

"So we sent the old dope after a gallon of beer and

pretzels. Soon as he left out the door Zarita grabbed me close as paper on the wall and started to dance. She danced so frantic, I could not keep up with her, so I turned her loose and let her go for herself. She had a great big old pocketbook on her arm and it were just a-swinging. Everybody else stopped dancing to watch Zarita, who always did want to be a show girl. She were really kicking up her heels then and throwing her hips from North to South. All of a sudden she flung up her arms and hollered, 'Yippeee-ee-ee-e!' whilst her pocketbook went flying through the air. When it hit the ceiling it busted wide open. Man, everything she had in it strewed out all over my floor as it come down.

" 'Lord have mercy!' Zarita said. 'Stop the music! Don't nobody move a inch. You might step on some of my personal belongings.'

"Just about then the downstairs doorbell rung nine times—my ring. I said, 'Somebody go down and let that guy in with the beer, while we pick up Zarita's stuff.'

"Zarita said, 'You help me, baby. The rest of you-all just stay where you are. I ain't acquainted with some of you folks and I don't want to lose nothing valuable.'

"Well, you know how many things a woman carries in her pocketbook. Zarita had lost them all, flung from 'one wall to the other of my room—compact busted open, powder spilt, mirror, key ring with seven keys, lipstick, handkerchief, deck of cards, black lace gloves, bottle opener, cigarette case, chewing gum, bromo-quinine box, small change, fountain pen, sun glasses, big old silver Bow-Dollar for luck, address books, fingernail file, three blue poker chips, matches, flask, also a shoehorn. Her perfume bottle broke against the radiator so my room smelt like womens, licker, mens, and a Night in Paris.

"Zarita was down on her hands and knees scrambling around for things, so I got down on my hands and knees, too.

" 'Baby,' she says to me, 'I believes my lipstick has rolled under your bed.'

"We both crawled under the bed to see. While we was under there, Zarita kissed me. She crawled out with the shoehorn and I crawled out with her lipstick—some of it on the side of my mouth. Just as I got up, there stood Joyce in my door with a package in her hand.

"Have you ever seen a man as dark as me turn red? I turned red, daddy-o! I opened my mouth to say 'Howdy-do?' but not a sound come out. Joyce had on her gold earrings and I could see they were shaking. But she did not raise her voice. She were too hurt.

"Zarita said, 'Why, Joyce, tip on in and enjoin my birthday. We don't mind. Just excuse my stuff flying all over the room. Me and Mr. Semple is having a ball.'

"Joyce looked at the black lace gloves, playing cards strewed all over the place, cigarette case, compact, poker chips, address book, powder, Bow-Dollar, and nail file on the floor with all them strange Negroes setting on the bed, in the window sill, on the dresser, everywhere but on the ceiling, and lipstick on my cheek. She did not say a word. She just turned her head away and looked like tears was aching to come to her eyes.

"I says, 'Joyce, baby, listen,' I says, 'I want a word with you.'

"She said, 'I come around here to bring you your yellow

rayon-silk shirt I ironed special for you for Sunday. Since your landlady said you was at home, she told me to bring it on upstairs myself. Here it is. I did not know you had company.'

"Just then that old down-home Negro come up with the beer yelling, 'Gangway! The stuff is here. Make room!' and he almost run over Joyce.

"Joyce says, 'Excuse me for being in your guests' way.'

"She turned to go. In facts, she went. I followed her down the steps but she did not turn her head. That loud-mouthed Zarita put the needle on Louis Jordan's bodacious 'Let the Good Times Roll,' and the ball were on again. When I got to the bottom of the steps, my landlady was standing like a marble statue.

"Landlady says, 'No decent woman approves of this.' Which is when Joyce started crying.

"Boy! My heart was broke because I hates to be misunderstood. I said, 'Joyce, I did not invite them parties here.'

"Joyce says, 'You don't need to explain to me, Jess Semple,' getting all formal and everything. She says, 'Now I have seen that woman with my own eyes in *your* bedroom with her stuff spread out every which-a-where just like she was home. And people I know from their looks could not be *your* friends because I never met any of them before—so they must be hers. Maybe Zarita lives with you. No wonder you giving a birthday party to which I am not invited. Good night, I am gone out of your life from now on. Enjoy yourself. Good night!'

"If she had fussed and raised her voice, I would not have felt so bad. But the sweet way she said, 'Enjoy your-

self,' all ladylike and sad and quiet, as if she was left out
of things, cut me to my soul. Joyce ought to know I would
not leave her out of nothing.

"I would of followed her in the street, but she said,
'Don't you come behind me!'

"The way she said it, I knowed she meant it. So I did
not go. When I turned back, there was my landlady. All
I said to that old battle-ax was, 'Go to hell!' I were so
mad at that woman for sending Joyce upstairs.

"She started yelling as I went on up the steps, but I
didn't hear a word she said. I knowed she was telling me
to find another room. But I did not care. All I wanted was
to lay eyes on Zarita, stop them damn records from playing, and get them low-down dirty no-gooders out of my
room. Which I did before you could say 'Jackie Robinson.'
But after they left, I could not sleep. It were a blue evening.

"Some of Zarita's stuff was still on the floor next day
when I went to work, so I gathered it up and brought it
down here to the bartender and left it for her. I do not
want to see Zarita no more again. The smell of that Night
in Paris water is still in my room. I'll smell it till the day
I die. But I don't care if I die right now. I don't know what
to say to Joyce. A man should not fool around a bad woman *no kind of way* when he's got a good woman to love.
They say, 'You never miss the water till the well runs dry.'
Boy, you don't know how I miss Joyce these last few days."

"Haven't you tried to see her?" I asked.

"Tried?" said Simple. "I phoned her seventeen times.
She will not answer the phone. I rung her bell. Nobody will
let me in. I sent her six telegrams, but she do not reply.

If I could write my thoughts, I would write her a letter, but I am no good at putting words on paper much. The way I feel now, nobody could put my feelings down nohow. I got the blues for true. I can't be satisfied. This morning I had the blues so bad, I wished that I had died. These is my bitter days. What shall I do?"

"I don't know."

"You never know anything important," said Simple. "All you know is to argue about race problems. Tonight I would not care if all the race problems in the world was to descend right on New York. I would not care if Rankin himself would be elected Mayor and the Ku Klux Klan took over the City Council. I would not care if Mississippi moved to Times Square. But nobody better not harm Joyce, I'm telling you, even if she has walked out of my life. That woman *is* my life, so nobody better not touch a hair of her head. Buddy-o, wait for me here whilst I walks by her house to see if there's a light in her window. I just want to know if she got home from work safe tonight."

"She's been getting home safely by herself all these years," I said. "Why are you so worried tonight?"

"Please don't start no whys and wherefores."

"I sympathize with you—still, there are always ameliorating circumstances."

"I don't know what that word means," said Simple, "but all that rates with me now is what to say to that girl—if I ever get a chance to say anything. If she does not come to the door when I ring this time, if I see a light I am going to holler."

"Since she lives on the third floor, you can hardly play Romeo and climb up," I said. "Still, I don't believe Joyce would relish having her name called aloud in the street."

"If she don't let me through the door, I will have to call her," said Simple. "I can explain by saying that I have lost my mind, that she has driv me crazy. And I will stand in front of her house all night if she don't answer."

"The law would probably remove you," I said.

"They would have to use force to do it," said Simple. "I wouldn't care if the polices broke my head, anyhow. Joyce done broke my heart."

"You've got it bad," I said.

"Worse than bad," moaned Simple. "Here, take this quarter and buy yourself a beer whilst you wait till I come back."

"I have some affairs of my own to attend to," I protested, "so I can't wait all night."

"I thought you was my ace-boy," he said as he turned away. "But everybody lets you down when trouble comes. If you can't wait, then don't. To hell with you! Don't!"

I started to say I would wait. But Simple was gone.

42

When a Man Sees Red

"I may not be a red," he said as he banged on the bar, "but sometimes I see red."

"What do you mean?"

"The way some of these people a man has to work for talks to a man, I see red. The other day my boss come saying to me that I was laying down on the job—when all I was doing was just thinking about Joyce. I said, 'What do you mean, laying down on the job? Can't you see me standing up?'

"The boss said, 'You ain't doing as much work as you used to do.'

"I said, 'A Dollar don't do as much buying for me as *it* used to do, so I don't do as much for a Dollar. Pay me some more money, and I will do more work.'"

"What did he say then?"

"He said, 'You talk like a red.'"

"I said, 'What do you mean, red?'"

"He said, 'You know what I mean—*red, communist.* After *all* this country has done for you Negroes, I didn't think you'd turn out to be a red.'

"I said, 'In my opinion, a man can be any color except yellow. I'd be yellow if I did not stand up for my rights.'

"The boss said, 'You have no right to draw wages and not work.'

"I said, 'I have *done* work, I *do* work, and I *will* work—but also a man is due to eat for his work, to have some clothes, and a roof over his head. For what little you are paying me, I can't hardly keep body and soul together. Don't you reckon I have a soul?' I said.

"Boss said, 'I have nothing to do with your soul. All I am concerned about is your work. You are talking like a communist, and I will not have no reds in my plant.'

"I said, 'It wasn't so long ago you would not have no Negroes in your plant. Now you won't have no reds. You must be color-struck!'

"That got him. That made him mad. He said, 'I have six Negroes working for me now.'

"I said, 'Yes, out of six hundred men. You wouldn't have them if you could've got anybody else during the war. And what kind of work do you give us? The dirty work! The cheapest wages! Maintenance department—which is just another way for saying *clean up*. You know you don't care nothing about us Negroes. You getting ready to fire me right now. Well, if you fire me, I will be a red for sure, because I see red this morning. *I will see the union, if you fire me,*' I said.

" 'Just go on and do your work,' he said, and walked off. But I was hot, pal! I'm telling you! But he did not look back. He didn't want to have no trouble out of that union."

"Now I know he will think you are a red," I said.

"Is it red to want to earn decent wages? Is it red to

want to keep your job? And not to want to take no stuff off a boss?"

"Don't yell at me," I said. "I'm not your boss. I didn't say a thing."

"No, but you implied," said Simple. "Just because you are not working for white folks, you implied."

"There you go bringing up the race issue again," I said. "I think you are too race-conscious."

"I am black," said Simple, "also I will be red if things get worse. But one thing sure, I will not be yellow. I will stand up for my rights till kingdom come."

"You'd better be careful or they will have you up before the Un-American Committee."

"I wish that old Southern chairman would send for me," said Simple. "I'd tell him more than he wants to know."

"For instance?" I said.

"For instant," said Simple, "I would say, 'Your Honery, I wish to inform you that I was born in America, I live in America, and long as I have been black, I been an American. Also I was a Democrat—but I didn't know Roosevelt was going to die.' Then I would ask them, 'How come you don't have any Negroes on your Un-American Committee?'

"And old Chairman Georgia would say, 'Because that is un-American.'

"Then I would say, 'It must also be un-American to run a train, because I do not see any colored engineers running trains. All I see Negroes doing on the railroads is sweeping out coaches and making beds. Is that American?'

"Old Chairman Georgia would say, 'Yes! Sweeping is American.'

"Then I would say, 'Well, I want to be un-American so I can run a train.'

"Old Chairman would say, 'You must be one of them Red Russians.'

" 'No, I ain't neither,' I would say. 'I was born down South, too, like you. But I do not like riding a Jim Crow car when I go home to Dixie. Also, I do not like being a Pullman porter *all the time*. Sometimes I want to *run* a train.'

" 'I know you are a Red Russian!' yells that old Chairman. 'You want to tear this country down!'

" 'Your Honery,' I says, 'I admit I would like to tear *half* of it down—the Southern half from Virginia to Mobile—just to build it over new. And when I built it over, I would put *you* in the Jim Crow car instead of me.'

" 'Hold that Negra in contempt of court!' yells Chairman Georgia.

" 'I thought you just said I was a Red Russian. Now here you go calling me a Negro. Which is I?'

" 'You're both,' says the Chairman.

" 'Why? Because I want to drive a train?'

" 'Yes,' yells the Chairman, 'because you want to drive a train! This is a white man's country. These is white men's trains! You cannot drive one. And down where I come from, neither can you ride in a WHITE coach.'

" 'You don't have any coaches for Red Russians,' I said.

" 'No,' yells the Chairman, 'but we will have them as soon as I can pass a law.'

" 'Then where would I ride?' I asked. 'In the COLORED coach or in the RED coach?'

" 'You will not ride nowhere,' yells the Chairman, 'because you will be in jail.'

" 'Then I will break your jail up,' I said, 'because I am entitled to liberty whilst pursuing happiness.'

" 'Contempt of court!' bangs the Chairman."

Just then the bartender flashed the lights off and on three times, indicating that it was time to close the bar, so I interrupted my friend's imaginary session of the Un-American Committee.

"Listen," I said, "you're intoxicated, and when you are intoxicated, you talk right simple. Things are not that simple."

"Neither am I," said Simple.

43

Race Relations

"Don't let's talk about it," he said when I asked him about Joyce. "Don't let's even mention her name. I can't stand it. I have tried every way I know to make up with that woman. But she must have a heart like a rock cast in the sea. I have also tried every way I know to forget her. But no dice. I cannot wear her off my mind. I've even taken up reading. This week I bought all the colored papers from the *Black Dispatch* to the *Afro-American,* trying to get a race-mad on, reading about lynchings, head-whippings, barrings-out, sharecroppers, cheatings, discriminations, and such. No dice. I have drunk five bottles of beer tonight and I'm still sober. Nothing has no effect. So let's just not talk about Joyce.

"There is a question, anyhow, I want to ask you because I wish to change the subject," said Simple.

"Them colored papers are full of stuff about Race Relations Committees functioning all over the country, and how they are working to get rid of the poll tax and to keep what few Negroes still have jobs from losing them, and such. But in so far as I can tell, none of them committees is taking up the real problem of race relations because I always thought *relations* meant being related. Don't it?

And to be related you have to have relations, don't you? But I don't hear nobody speaking about us being kinfolks. All they are talking about in the papers is poll taxes and jobs."

"By relations, I take it that you mean intermarriage? If that is what you mean, nobody wants to talk about that. That is a touchy subject. It is also beside the point. Equal rights and fair employment have nothing to do with inter-marriage."

"Getting married," said Simple, "is also a equal right."

"You do not want to marry a white woman, do you?" I asked.

"I do not," said Simple, "but I figure some white woman might want to marry me."

"You'd better not let Joyce hear you talking like that," I said. "You know colored women do not like the idea of intermarriage at all."

"I know they don't," said Simple. "Neither do white men. But if the races are ever going to relate, they must also mate, then you will have race relations."

"Race relations do not necessarily have to be on so racy a basis," I said. "At any rate, speaking about them in such a manner only infuriates the South. It makes Southerners fighting mad."

"I do not see why it should infuriate the South," said Simple, "because the South has always done more relat-ing than anybody else. There are more light-skinned Ne-groes in the South whose pappy was a white man than there is in all the rest of this whole American country."

"True," I said, "many colored people are related to white people down South. But *some* relationships are private matters, whereas things like equal job opportunities, an unsegregated army, the poll tax, and no more Jim Crow cars affect everybody, in bed or out. These are the things Race Relations Committees are trying to deal with all over the country. It would only complicate the issues if they brought up intermarriage."

"Issues are complicated already," said Simple. "Why, I even got white blood in me myself, dark as I am. And in some colored families I know personally down South, you can hardly tell high yellows from white."

"My dear fellow," I said, "the basic social issues which I am talking about are not to be dealt with on a family basis, but on a mass basis. All Negroes, with white blood in them or not, in fact, everybody of whatever parentage, ought to have the right to vote, to live a decent life, and to have fair employment."

"Also to relate," said Simple.

"I keep telling you, race relations do not have anything to do with that kind of relating!"

"If they don't," said Simple, "they are not relations."

"Absurd," I said. "I simply will not argue with you any more. You're just as bad as those Southerners who are always bringing up intermarriage as a reason for *not* doing anything. What you say is entirely beside the point."

"The point must have moved then," said Simple.

"We are not talking about the same thing at all," I said patiently. "I am talking about fair employment, and you are talking about . . ."

"Race relations," said Simple.

44

Possum, Race, and Face

"Since you just came in, how come you've got to go so soon? If you was a good buddy, you'd wait until I have one more beer," said Simple about two A.M. Saturday night in the crowded bar. "I have to get up kinder early in the morning myself, at least by noon. I am going to have Sunday dinner with Joyce! We have made up, man! And she is cooking especially for me. I wish I could invite you, but I can't, 'cause Joyce just invited me *alone.*"

"I'm happy to hear you're reunited," I said. "In truth, I am delighted. How did you two effect your reconciliation?"

"We just couldn't stand not to see each other no longer."

"Who gave in first?" I asked. "You or Joyce?"

"We both gave in at once, man. You know how those things is. I forgived her—and she forgived me. Now she is cooking again—and I have got my appetite back."

"What are you going to eat tomorrow?"

"Chicken, since it is Sunday," said Simple, "but I wish it were possum."

"Possum! Now I know you are intoxicated. Where on earth can you get a possum in New York?"

"As many Negroes as there are in Harlem, there ought

to be at least one possum around in the fall of the year. Listen, man, tonight if I had a lantern and a hound dog and a gun, and if there was a persimmon tree on Sugar Hill and that possum .was up that tree, I'll bet you I would get myself a possum this very night. I bet on that!"

"So you used to hunt possum down home?"

"He could be up a nut tree, too, or whatever kind of tree he was up, me and my hound would find him out and bring him down," declared Simple.

"Do you suppose Joyce knows how to cook a possum?" I asked.

"She might not admit it," said Simple, "but I'll bet you if I brought her one, she would not give it up for silver nor gold. Between her and an oven, that possum would come out good. But I don't reckon nobody in America could cook a possum like my Uncle Tige. The way Uncle Tige cooked a possum, man, you would not want nothing better on this earth, *never!*"

"I never heard tell of your Uncle Tige before. Who was he?"

"I lived with him and Aunt Minnie for a time when I were ten, eleven, twelve."

"You sure lived with a lot of different relatives."

"I was passed around," explained Simple. "When I were a child, I was passed around. But not even with Grandma Arcie did I eat so good. Not *no* place did I eat so good as with Uncle Tige. Him and Aunt Minnie both liked to eat. They both could cook. And sometimes they would see who could outcook the other. Chitterlings—man, don't talk! Hog jowl, hog maw, pig tails, pig feets! They tasted like the Waldorf-Astoria *ought* to taste—but

I know it don't. Corn dumplings, turnip greens, young onions! Catfish, buffalo fish, also perch! Cabbage with cayenne pepper! Tripe! Chime bones and kraut! On Sunday two hens stuffed with sage dressing! Also apple dumpling! Umm-m-huh!

"When they sent me back to my Aunt Lucy, I was so big and fat the schoolteacher looked at me and said, 'Boy, how come you're only in the fourth grade? Big as you is, you ought to be in the low ninth.'

"I had done et so much cracklin' bread I was oozing out grease and so many hominy grits with gravy till my hair was oily and laid down just like a Indian's. I did not have to use no Murray's Pomade then. But that was long ago. And I have not et like that since I come to New York. I would give all the ducks, chickens, and turkeys in the world for a possum.

"A possum for Sunday dinner, man, would be perfect, cooked like my Uncle Tige used to cook him. First singe him in hot ashes, then clean him, then bake him—and that possum all stuffed with apples and fruits and pineapples with great big old red yams laid around his sides, plenty of piccalilli and chowchow and watermelon-rind pickles setting in little cut-glass dishes all around the table. And a great big old jug of hard cider to drink along with that possum. Aw, man, Sunday would be perfect then! But since we will not have a possum, I will have a good dinner tomorrow right on. Joyce is making hot biscuits. And if there is anything I like in this world, it is biscuits."

"Me, too," I said.

"I also like beer," said Simple.

"Then why don't you set us up?"

"Because I haven't got a dime left. I stashed my money home this week since I intend to take Joyce out to a show or something every night now that we made up. But if I ever get hold of a possum in Harlem, you will get some of it. You are my friend."

"Give us a beer, Tony," I said. But the bartender didn't hear me with the juke box going.

"Sometimes I set and remember when I were nothing but a child," Simple continued. "In this noisy old bar I set sometimes and remember when I were a child, and I would not want to be a child again. But some things about it was good—like possum. There was other things I don't like to remember. Some of them things keep coming back to me sometimes when I set in this bar and look in the bottom of my beer glass and there ain't no more beer."

"Another round, Tony!"

"When I were a growing boy and lived with my Aunt Lucy, I used to hear the old folks saying, 'Take all this world and gimme Jesus!' Aunt Lucy were a great Christian, so she used to go to church all the time, facts, she were a pillar of the church. It was her determination to go to Beulah Land, and I do believe she went. In this life she had very little to look forward to—except some more hard work. So no wonder she said, 'Take all this world—but gimme Jesus!' Well, the white folks have taken this world."

"What makes you think that?"

"The earth don't belong to me," said Simple. "Not even no parts of it. This bar does not belong to me. It belongs to Italians. The house I live in does not belong to me. It belongs to Jews. The place I work at belongs to an Irishman. He can fire me any time he gets ready. The insurance I'm in belongs to white folks. And I reckon the cemetery I'll be buried in belongs to them, too. The only thing I own is the clothes on my back—and I bought them from a white store."

"You could at least belong to a colored insurance," I said.

"My mama put me in the Metropolitan when I were knee-high to a duck, and I never did get around to changing my policy," said Simple. "But you are getting me off my point—which is that this *world* belongs to white folks."

"Have you been all over the world?"

"No," said Simple, "but I reads. I listens to world news on the radio every day. I am no dumbbell. I hear all about the Dutch in Java, the Americans in Japan, and the English in Africa, where I hear they have Jim Crow cars. Don't tell me o'fays don't own the world."

"That doesn't necessarily mean they are going to keep it forever," I said, competing with the music on the juke box and the noise at the bar. "The colonial system is bound to come to an end."

"When?" asked Simple.

"Before long. The British Empire is on its last legs. The Dutch haven't got much left."

"But the crackers still have Mississippi, Georgia, Alabama, and Washington, D.C.," said Simple.

"I admit that, but when we start voting in greater numbers down South, and using the ballot as we ought to up North, they won't be as strong as they might have been."

"I hope I live to see that day," said Simple. "Anyhow,

the next time I go to church, I am going to pray for the Lord to give back some of this world to colored folks."

"I am glad you intend to go to church. But what you ought to pray is *not* to have the world split up between colored and white nations, but instead, to have the spirit of co-operation enter into *everybody's* soul so that we all could build a decent world together."

"If I was to really pray what is in my mind," said Simple, "the Lord would shut up His ears and not listen to me at all. If I was to pray what is in my mind, I would pray for the Lord to wipe white folks off the face of the earth. Let 'em go! Let 'em go! *And let me rule awhile!*"

"I'll bet you would do a fine job of ruling," I said sarcastically.

"I would do better than they have done. First place, with white folks wiped out, I would stop charging such high rents—so my landlady could charge *me* less. Second place, I would stop hoarding up all the good jobs for white folks—so I could get ahead myself. Third place, I would make the South behave. Fourth place, I would let Asia and Africa go free, and I would build them all schools and air-cooled movies and barbecue pits—and give everybody enough to eat, including possum. Then I would say, 'If you-all colored folks in Africa and Asia and elsewhere, including Harlem, don't behave yourselves, I will drop an atom bomb on you and wipe you out, too—just like the Lord wiped out the white folks!' I would make everybody behave themselves."

"In other words, you would repeat the same old mistake of force and violence that the white nations have been guilty of," I said.

"Except that I would *force* people to be *good,* and get educated, and run themselves, and enjoy Lena Horne and Bing Crosby, and eat aplenty. I would *make* people do *right.* I would not let them do wrong."

"You would do more than God is doing," I said.

"Man, I would be *a hell,*" cried Simple, "a natural hell!"

"I think you must be drunk," I said. "Stop yelling so loud, or that white bartender will think you're a disgrace to the race."

"Oh," sighed Simple, "there are certainly a lot of disadvantages in being colored. The way that juke box is blaring, a body has to yell. Yet you can't even holler out loud without somebody saying, 'Shsss-ss-s! Don't be so rowdy in front of white folks.' You can't even get drunk and walk staggle-legged down the street without somebody accusing you of disgracing the race. I think Negroes should have as much right to get drunk and misbehave in front of anybody as the next person has, without somebody always throwing it up in our faces about disgracing the race."

Simple paused for a long drink of beer, gulped, took a deep breath, and went on.

"If a colored man even gambles a little penny ante and the place gets raided, there is a big headline in the papers:

HARLEM VICE DEN RAIDED

"But at them downtown clubs they gambles hundreds of dollars every night, never do get raided, and nobody calls them a vice den. But just let a colored man roll one roll—and he is a disgrace to the race. Or take murder and manslaughter, for instant. A white man can kill his wife, cut her up, put her in a trunk, ship her to California, and never get her body out of the baggage room, yet nobody talks about he is a disgrace to the white race. But just let a Negro carve somebody once lightly with a small knife and the papers say:

BIG BLACK BUCK RUNS AMUCK

"Then everybody in Harlem says, 'What a shame for a Negro to act that way,' and 'How is the Race ever gonna get anywhere?' Why, hundreds of white folks kills hundreds of other white folks every day, and nobody says, 'What a shame for a white man to act like that.'"

"Well, being a minority race," I said, "we have to save face. We have to act better than white people act, so they won't brand us as being worse."

"Being worse?" cried Simple, topping Louis Jordan's loudest riff on the juke box. "How could colored folks be worse? Hitler was white and he killed up more folks in *three years* than all the Negroes put together have kilt since B.C. Just look at all them colored mens Southerners have lynched and burnt! How could we be any worse? But me—if I even have one *small* penknife in my pocket that I never use, and I get caught and locked up, they fingerprint me, take my picture and put it in the papers with a big headline:

HARLEMITE BRANDISHES WEAPON

and make out like I am a black disgrace to the U.S.A. I do not think that is right, and if I was ruling the world it would not be. I think I should have as much right as the next one to be a disgrace—if I want to be—without any-body talking about my race."

"*Nobody* has a right to be a disgrace," I said. "That is where you are wrong. I do not appreciate your argument."

"I don't mean people *ought* to kill and murder," said Simple. "But let's get back to what I started with, getting drunk. I see plenty of white men get on the busses drunk, and nobody says that a white man is a disgrace to his race. But just let a colored man get on the bus drunk! Everybody says, 'Tuc-tuc-tuc!' The white folks say, 'That's just like a Negro.' And the colored folks say, 'It's a shame. A disgrace to our group.' Yet the poor man hasn't done a thing but get drunk."

"Nobody, white or colored, has any business getting on a bus or streetcar drunk," I said. "If you are drunk, you should take a taxi home. Drunks are nuisances, staggering around and talking out of turn—like you when you are high. I do not agree with you this evening."

"If you agreed, there would be no point in having an argument," said Simple, pushing back his glass.

"There is not very much point to *your* argument," I said.

"Except," said Simple solemnly, "that I think colored folks should have the same right to get drunk as white folks."

"That is a very ordinary desire," I said. "You ought to want to have the right to be President, or something like that."

"Very few men can become President," said Simple. "And only one at a time. But almost anybody can get drunk. Even I can get drunk."

"Then you ought to take a taxi home, and not get on

the bus smelling like a distillery," I said, "staggering and disgracing the race."

"I keep trying to tell you, if I was white, wouldn't nobody say I was disgracing no race!"

"You definitely are not white," I said.

"You got something there," said Simple. "Lend me taxi fare and I will ride home."

45

A Letter from Baltimore

As I walked into Paddy's, there stood Simple grinning from ear to ear. He greeted me like a long-lost brother, pulling me toward the bar as he announced, "This evening the beers are on me and I have the where-with-all to pay for two rounds and a half, so pick up and drink down."

"What, may I ask, is the occasion for this sudden conviviality? Tonight is not Saturday."

"No," said Simple, "but it is a new day right on, a new week, and a new year. They say a man's life changes every seven years. I am in the change. Here, read this letter that I found laying on the radiator in the hall this evening when I come in that I know my landlady tried to peer through the envelope. It's from my wife, Isabel."

"I have no desire to pry into your personal correspondence," I said.

"Read it, man, read it," urged Simple. "Desire or not, read it. I want to hear it in words *out loud* what Mrs. Semple says—because I cannot believe my eyes. Unfold it, go ahead."

"She writes a nice clear hand," I said, "big round letters. You can tell this woman is a positive character. I see she's still in Baltimore, too. Well, here goes:

Dear Mr. Semple:

Jess, at last I have found a man who loves me enough to pay for my divorce, which is more than you was ever willing to do and you are my husband. Now, listen, this man is a mail clerk that owns two houses, one of which he has got rented and the other one he needs somebody to take care of it. His first wife being dead so he wants me for his second. He knows I have been married once before and am still married in name only to you as you have not been willing to pay for the legal paper which grants freedom from our entanglement. This man is willing to pay for it, but he says I will have to file the claim. He says he will get a lawyer to furnish me grounds I have to swear on and that you also have to swear on unless you want to contest. *I do not want no contest*, you hear me? All I want is my divorce, since I have found a nice man, willing to marry me and pay for it, too. I am writing to find out if you will please not make no contest out of this because he has never done nothing to you, only do you a favor by bearing the expenses of the grounds that rightly belong to a husband. Let me hear from you this evening as he has already passed the point where he could wait.

Once sincerely yours but not now,
Isabel

"I suppose you would have no intention of cross-filing," I said.

"I would not cross that wife of mine no kind of way," said Simple, "with a file nor otherwise. My last contest with that woman was such that the police had to protect me. So that man can have her. He can have her! I do not even want a copy of the diploma."

"A divorce paper does not look like a diploma," I said.

"I knew a woman once who framed her divorce and hung it on the wall," said Simple. "But if my wife serves *me* with one, I will throw it out."

"That would render it invalid," I said, "also null and void. You will have to sign all the papers and mail them back to Baltimore so the proceedings can go through."

"Just so they get out of my sight," said Simple. "Joyce would not want no other woman's divorce papers hanging around. If she did, Joyce could have bought them papers herself by now. I gave her the opportunity."

"I am always puzzled as to why you have been so unwilling to pay for your own divorce," I said.

"I told Isabel when we busted up that she had shared my bed, she had shared my board, my licker, and my Murray's, but that I did not intend to share another thing with her from that day to this, not even a divorce. That is why I would not pay for it. Let that other man pay for it and they can share it together."

"But it will free you to marry Joyce," I said.

"Joyce will be free to marry me, you mean."

"Joyce is not being divorced from anyone. You are the one who is being divorced."

"Which means I will no longer be free, then," said Simple. "I will be married again before the gold seal is hardly out from under the stamper."

"That will be good for you. Perhaps you will settle down, stay home, stop running around nights."

"I will," said Simple, "because I will have a home to stay at. I will not have to live in bars to keep from looking at my landlady in the face."

"Maybe married you can save a little money and get somewhere in the world."

"Them would be my best intentions," said Simple. "Facts is, I always did have ambitions. When I were a little boy in Virginia, my grandma told me to hitch my wagon to a star."

"Did you try?"

"I did," said Simple, "but it must have been a dog-star."

"Well, now things will be different. Joyce is a good girl. You love her and she loves you, so this time you should make a go of it. And I will dance at your wedding."

"You will be my best man," said Simple.

"Well, of course, I'd be delighted—but—but maybe you'd like a relative or some other more intimate friend for your best man. After all, Joyce doesn't know me very well."

"*I* know you," said Simple, "which is enough. As many beers as you have bought me right here at this bar, and as often as you lent me a buck when I was trying to make the week, you deserve to be my best man. So no arguments! Now that my luck is turned, daddy-o, you'll be there at the finish."

"Thanks, old man," I said. "Certainly you seem to be coming out ahead at last—a *free* divorce from a wife you don't like, no contest, no expenses, and, all but for the formalities, a new wife you love."

"I *am* coming out ahead for once," said Simple, "which just goes to prove what's in that little old toast I learned from my Uncle Tige. Listen fluently:

When you look at this life you'll find
It ain't nothing but a race.
If you can't be the winning horse,
Son, at least try to place.

"I believe I have placed—so let's drink to it."

"You have won," I said.

"Providing that Negro in Baltimore keeps his promise to my wife. If he don't, as sure as my name is Simple, I will go down there and beat his head."

"Do you mean to say you'd lay hands on your first wife's second husband?"

"Listen! I married Isabel for better or for worse. She couldn't do no better than to get a free divorce," said Simple. "That man made my wife a promise. *He better not betray her.* If he does, he'll have me to contend with because I dare him to stand in *my* way. I'll fix him! Just like that toast says:

If they box you on the curve, boy,
Jockey your way to the rail,
And when you get on the inside track—
Sail! ... Sail! ... Sail!
In a race, daddy-o,
One thing you will find—
There ain't NO *way to be out in front*
Without showing your tail
To the horse behind."

"One regrets," I said, "that, after all, life is a conflict."

"I leave them regrets to you," said Simple.

About the Author

LANGSTON HUGHES *began to write at fourteen, when he was elected class poet of his grammar-school graduating class in Lincoln, Illinois. His first printed poems appeared the following year in the* Central High School *magazine at Cleveland, Ohio, where he was a member of the track team and a captain in the school military reserve unit. His first work to be published in a national magazine appeared the year after his graduation from high school. Since then he has published thirteen books and many stories, articles, plays, poems, opera librettos, and songs, among them those for the musical version of* Street Scene. *One of his plays,* Mulatto, *ran for a year on Broadway and was recently performed as an opera at Columbia University. His books have been translated into French, Spanish, German, Dutch, Chinese, Japanese, and Uzbek, and he has been awarded Guggenheim and Rosenwald Fellowships, as well as an honorary grant from the American Academy of Arts and Letters.*

Simple Speaks His Mind *began as a series of stories written especially for readers of the* Chicago Defender— *largely average nonliterary American Negroes. Mr. Hughes writes, "I live in the heart of Harlem. I have also lived in the heart of Paris, Madrid, Shanghai, and Mexico City. The people of Harlem seem not very different from others, except in language. I love the color of their language; and, being a Harlemite myself, their problems and interests are my problems and interests."*